I0708382

OUTSTANDING PRAISE FOR
THE RELUCTANT CONDUCTOR

<u>A Page Turner</u>
The Reluctant Conductor is most definitely a page turner. It is also timely and beautifully written. The cost of love and war and… the power of music. While the book is set during and after the war, WWll, it could've been written yesterday with all that is going on in the world – Ukraine and Russia. The authors, Turner and Gorbaty, have written a powerful historical novel. The hero, Elazar, a violinist, is both tender and audacious; his journey is filled with all of life – love, pain, devastation, and hope.

— **Amy Ferris** is a screenwriter, influencer, badass and author of Mighty Gorgeous: A Little Book About Messy Love.

<u>Old Fashioned Storytelling. Deliciously Escapist</u>
This is storytelling from the Old World, a panoramic sweep through the tortured times and people of Eastern Europe. It is the story of Elazar, a young Jewish violinist in search of redemptive love and transportive music, in a world full of ugly bigotry and hate. Drifting back and forth between Uzbekistan and the Ukraine between 1922 and 1944, our hero navigates wedding-night steam rooms and birch-branch floggings; rivers of refugees and rivers of blood; lice and typhoid and refugee tent camps; horse-drawn carriage rides through betrayal and death and

flattened shtetls; and the small luxuries of the desperate, a simple plate of chicken and cabbage. But always, always, the ebb and flow of music, weaving in and out of a life lost in the terrifying wilderness, searching for family and home. Does our hero find what he is yearning for? Read the book to find out. I picked it up and had to find out what happened to se to Elazar, a narrator I cared about.

— **Richard C. Morais**, author of the New York Times and international best-selling novel *The Hundred Foot Journey.*

<u>Rich Portrait With Fascinating Historical Accuracy</u>
Tim Turner and Moisey Gorbaty have written an emotionally powerful novel that captures Jewish life in the Soviet Union, before during and after WWII. The Reluctant Conductor depicts the hardship, oppression and hope of the era, combining the engaging storytelling of a novel against the turbulent history of the era.

In addition to finding it a great read, I particularly enjoyed the history as it enabled me to better understand the situation in Ukraine and with Russia today. — **Sean Strub**, author of Body Counts, A Memoir of Activism, Sex and Survival.

<u>Love Outlasts War</u>
This is a short, fast-paced novel about a Jewish family trying to survive WWII in the Soviet Union. The first section of the book is set earlier, in the 1920s, and focuses on the protagonist's love story. There also are adjustments to be made as their home town becomes part of the USSR — and the effects of communism

are felt. Through it all, the characters focus on family. The setup works because, as war breaks out years later when Germany invades, the reader is heavily invested in the characters and the family they built together. From there it is a flight for survival, which is grueling but told in spare detail that should not trigger sensitive readers. The post-war section ofz the book brings many elements full circle, with satisfying effect.

— **Dawn**

Touching Novel of a Jewish Family's Flight Across War-Torn Europe

The authors touchingly handle themes of loss and belonging as they dramatize, in brisk and poignant scenes, the everyday yet extraordinary experiences of refugee life… Despite the complexity of the political instability of the era, The Reluctant Conductor is at heart an elemental story of one family caught up in the larger context of geopolitics and genocide, a humane examination of the cost in individual lives of ancient hatreds.

— *BookLife*

A Moving Family Tale with a Strong Cast That Readers Will Love.

"An indomitable man guides his Jewish family through the horrors of World War II in Eastern Europe... Turner and Gorbaty's engaging debut novel is promising and timely, considering what is going on in the protagonist's part of the world. Elazar, the narrator, carries the story and will win readers over right from the start… A scene involving the family member fighting typhus is beautiful and poignant (Dickens would approve)…"

— *Kirkus Reviews*

ALSO BY TIM TURNER

PLAYS

Ties
Nevermore
Prairie Fire
Chicken and Fish
Out Late
High Time

LIBRETTO

Tortilla Flat

SCREENPLAYS

Early Returns
Out Late
High Time

THE RELUCTANT CONDUCTOR

A NOVEL

TIM TURNER & MOISEY GORBATY

Bessarabian Publishers
Los Angeles, CA
turner-gorbaty.com

First Edition: November 2023

ISBN 979-8-9899124-1-4

Library of Congress Control Number: 2023915666

Cover design by Joshua George Shaji

Printed in the United States of America

FOR ME

UKRAINE
RUSSIA
GEORGIA
TURKEY
BLACK SEA
KOTOVSK
KALARASH
DUBASARI
KISHINEV
ODESA
BOLGRAD
DNIPRO
DONETSK
MARIUPOL
ROSTOV-ON-DON
VOLGOGRAD
KHASAVYU

UKRAINE
MOLDOVA
ROMANIA
KOTOVSK
KALARASH
DUBASARI
KISHNEV
ODESA
BOLGRAD
KAZAKHSTAN
GURYEV
UZBEKISTAN
KATTAKURGAN
CASPIAN SEA
BAKU
TURKMENBASHI
TURKMENISTAN
IRAN
N
NW
NE
W
E
SW
NE
S

PROLOGUE

7 July 1922 — My papa is flourishing his pipe like a conductor's baton. Smoke wafts through the dining room as he finishes his usual diatribe with: "It's all about family," then stares at me. I squirm like a violinist who has lost his rhythm. "Are you with us, Elazar?"

It's Shabbat, Friday evening, I'm twenty-two years old, and I'm home in Kalarash poking at the sodden remains of my chicken and matzah balls. I unloaded boxcars full of rocks, bricks and lumber all week with my brother Herschel and I hurt all over. Mama gives me a calming smile as she rises to clear the table. Sarah snaps to and helps.

"It's a complex arrangement," I say.

"Keep practicing," he says.

When I was three, we lived in Kishinev, about fifty kilometers to the southeast. During Passover/Easter weekend that year, the Christians waged a pogrom on the city's Jewish population. In our case, that means they ransacked our store, set our house on fire, murdered my sister, and my baby brother and they threw me off the roof.

For real.

While pogroms have happened for hundreds of years all over Europe – from Barcelona to Prague – this happened in the 20th century. Initially, it was a global scandal wherein politicians from America and all over were outraged and demanded justice. But punishment for the perpetrators came to little or no avail, and because countless, more outrageous atrocities have since occurred, to most of the world, the Kishinev Pogrom of 1903 has been swept under the carpet.

Not to us.

I don't know how or why any of us survived but that's why papa and mama, Toiva and Polina Gershovich, uprooted our family, packed up the business, and fled to this shtetl—this Jewish prison.

In Kalarash, life is simple. Most people are Jewish. We speak Yiddish. Herschel and I went to *yeshiva*, Jewish school, where we studied Hebrew, the Torah and Talmud, from which the rabbis taught us to live every day like it's your last. To that end, they say number one: have some fun, two: try to do some good, and three: don't screw anyone over too badly, as you may be meeting your maker that evening. So that's what we do. We go to the Synagogue, we celebrate Yom Kippur, Hanukkah, Passover, whatever, and nobody tries to kill us.

Not everybody here is Jewish. It's only been in recent memory that it's become a shtetl. There are a couple of monasteries nearby that were built in the 1700s, even a cathedral, and with that, amicable *goys*, non-Jews, who speak our region's book-end languages: Romanian and Ukrainian. Unlike in Kishinev, papa maintains a low-key presence here—he's not politically active. But with the farmers, dairymen and former vintners, our family is respected, and we socialize amongst one another.

Papa is fifty-three, and while he finds solace here, giving up our store, our house, our horses, and his whole life in Kishinev has taken its toll. He has trouble sleeping, he has a stiff lower back, and he treats Herschel and me like strivers. Yet, in nineteen years he's fought and clawed his way back. We still don't have horses, but we own our properties—our house and the store—and we pay taxes to the King of Romania.

Mama is fifty-one, and to this day I don't know all the details, but there is no question that the pogrom and the exodus from Kishinev scarred her for life. She looks old for her age and while she's loving and ultra-protective, there is deep-seated pain in her facial expressions, the husky tone of her voice and the hunched over way in which she walks.

While our family has managed to rebuild our life out here in the heartland of Bessarabia, the big downside for me is there are very few girls my age, and I've known all of them since I was a child. I've dated several, gone through the usual coming-of-age milestones, but now dating any potential female mate in Kalarash seems incestuous.

In my life there is percussion in day-to-day work, the rise and fall of the sun, and the coming and going of the seasons. There is rhythm in family, eating meals, and celebrating holidays; but alas, there is no beauty, no high notes, no intimacy… no melody.

First Movement
Chapter 1

11 July 1922 — After yeshiva I knew one thing: I didn't want to become a rabbi. I wanted to move anywhere fun – Kishinev, Odesa, Bucharest, or Kyiv.

"And do what?" papa asks. "Become a furrier? A jeweler?"

"A musician," I say.

"Right," papa says. "And play weddings, birthdays, and bar mitzvahs?"

Our family actually is a band. Papa plays accordion and conducts, mama's a dynamo on the clarinet, I wail on the violin, Herschel beats the drums, and we all sing. After dinner, we entertain each other playing Jewish klezmer songs—Hava Nagila and the like.

"That's not a job, Elazar," papa says.

"And you have to work nights," mama adds. "Don't. You'll thank me when you have a family."

"Let's all move back to Kishinev… Move the store back," I plead.

Mama and papa both glare at me and shake their heads.

"It's a much bigger market," I say. "We could make more money. The Rezniks moved back and they're not dead."

"Forget it," papa decrees.

I'm tempted to go on my own, to pursue my musical ambitions, but it would kill mama and I'd feel guilty for the rest of my life. Papa's words ring in my head, *"It's all about family."*

I must stay in the shtetl, get married, have kids, grandkids, great grandkids… and spend Shabbat—and every other holiday—with my family. Oy.

In the four years since I finished yeshiva, I have worked for papa at *Gershovich's Hardware and Tack.* We have a great location. The back of the property sits next to the railroad track, which is perfect for receiving supplies. We're just southeast of downtown near a busy corner where the road from Bravicea meets Strada Alexandru cel Bun, the main road through Kalarash.

Back in Kishinev, family lore has it that papa was all things to the community: a steward, railway agent, fertilizer salesman, social adviser, character reference, politician, lodge master, and general community 'obliger.' The front doors and porch pillars served as bulletin boards. There was an open area around the stove where the patrons gathered for gabbling, yarn spinning, chewing, and smoking.

Maybe that's why some goys hated him; he had too much power, was too enviable, and too many people owed him money.

Here in Kalarash, we focus on 'hard' lines, including lumber, bricks, and stones, as well as builders' hardware including tools, agricultural implements, machinists' supplies, cutlery, and saddlers' hardware. We accept Romanian leu, but we also barter with everything from gold, gemstones, beeswax, or alcohol for all goods.

Papa manages the store, does the buying, and attends to important clients. Like on the accordion, he plays rhythm and melody and, in every way—manifested mostly in facial expressions, gestures, and vocal inflection—conducts our family and the business.

Mama cooks, cleans, runs the cash register, and keeps the books. For her, being a clarinetist and an accountant are a good match because she likes details, she's bright, loves a good laugh under the right circumstances, and hasn't minded a few squeaks along the way to mastering her instrument.

Herschel, who is twenty-four—two years older and now two inches shorter than I—is consistent and content to sit in the back of the orchestra. He has thinning, reddish hair, is married to his childhood sweetheart, Sarah, and they have an adorable son, Shimon, who is one year old. He's happy to be a husband, dad, and the family percussionist; he's always there keeping rhythm and at crescendo moments, comes in with a crash of the cymbals.

Sarah? She's twenty-three, a bit plain looking, and has no voice and no musical talent, but she's a meticulous housekeeper, a good cook, and a loving mother. All bands need solid stagehands.

Between her, Herschel, and me, we do the heavy work. We unload supplies as they come in on the train, we stock the shelves, help customers load their buggies, and we keep the place clean.

I used to be the underling, but as of late it has become clear that I am, literally and figuratively, the first-chair violinist in the family. Not only am I more physically able but Herschel also has a bad limp; one of the marauders in the pogrom deliberately snapped both bones below the knee on his right leg and it never healed right. Moreover, I have a better mind for business and more charm dealing with customers, so I'm the lead performer up front with papa, who is grooming me to become the conductor.

But the thing is, that grooming could go on for decades, and in the meantime, papa can be a real prick. I can't do anything right. No matter what I do, he tells me to do the opposite. I turn right, he tells me to turn left. I look up, he tells me to look down. I stock a shelf one way, he wants it another. I play my violin, but it's never right. Sometimes, I want to shove my bow up his ass.

It's afternoon, our cherry tree is in full bloom, and Herschel and I take a break from chopping firewood all day in preparation for winter. Hershel goes on an extended visit to the outhouse doing God knows what, and I go into the house to quench my thirst.

Mama greets me with a glass of lemonade. The postman came earlier, and as I drink my beverage, mama lingers over a printed card.

I have found that the biggest moments in life, the ones that change everything, usually catch you by surprise. You might not even recognize them as they happen. Mama's eyes sparkle as she says, "This came this afternoon."

She hands me the open envelope, which is addressed to the Gershovich Family.

"What's this?" I ask.

"Read it," she says.

I pull out the card. "You are invited to the wedding of Leonid Reznik and Anna…" I look up. "Cousin Leo? Mazel Tov! I didn't know he was engaged."

Leo and I have been best friends forever. His papa—mama's brother—had a furniture manufacturing business in Kalarash, and papa supplied them with materials. A couple of years ago, his papa's business bought out another furniture company and they moved back to Kishinev.

"Do you want to go?" mama asks.

My mind flits like a swarm of titmice. "Yeah," I say.

"Weddings are a great place to meet girls," she says.

"I love Leo. So, are we all going? As a family? Where will we stay?"

"Woah, slow down," mama says. "I already ran this by your papa. This is a busy time of year, and someone must run the store. In case you never noticed, Toiva doesn't cook. Herschel and Sarah have their new baby."

"So?" I ask.

"You could go by yourself. Stay with the Rezniks."

CHAPTER 2

5 Aug. 1922 — Early on a Saturday morning, less than a month later, I board the train from Kalarash to Kishinev. My stomach is fluttery. I've barely eaten for days. Once again, in my head I am narrating my experience as if to my grandchildren. "And then grandpa got on the train for the ride to meet your grandma for the first time. He was nervous, but also excited. Somehow, he just knew that this weekend would be life-changing."

Wheels screech, causing me to lurch forward as my train comes to a halt. I jump up before the other passengers pack the aisle and secure my violin case, put on my black fedora, grab my suitcase, and hop off the train. In my wake, the other passengers disembark toward factories, warehouses, a hospital, and a wooded park. In the distance, church bells chime nine times.

I look around for Leo, but in the growing crowd, every face looks strange. I catch up with a tall, fit Jewish guy but… it isn't him. Just as I start to grow concerned, a low voice calls out, "Elazar! Lazar!"

We make eye contact and hurry toward one another. Then I put down my suitcase and violin and we shake hands, then give each other a hug. When we were going through puberty, we used to masturbate together. It was nothing; we were just kids experimenting, but we've always been close. We learned to play violin together – we practiced for hours on end - and we were *chavrusas*, study partners, in yeshiva. Lately, we haven't seen each other in almost two years. He's grown a sparce beard and filled out a few kilos, but it's as if we saw each other the day before.

"Thanks for meeting my train. I really appreciate it. I mean, you are getting married tonight. Today must be really busy," I say.

"Yes, there's a lot going on, but I'm glad you're here," he says, looking at my burden. "Can I help you carry anything?"

"No. No, I'm fine," I say.

He snatches my violin and says, "I'll carry this. Have you been practicing?"

"A lot. And it keeps me balanced. How about you?"

"Not so much. I've been busy with work. And Anna."

"Excuses. Excuses."

I pick up my suitcase and we start to walk.

"Are you going to play tonight?" Leo asks.

"I was hoping to."

"That would be fantastic. What are you going to play?"

"It's a surprise," I say.

"Even better. God, it's good to see you," he says.

"It's good to see you," I say.

"No really," Leo says, and punches me in the arm.

"If you have things you have to do today, I will happily amuse myself. I don't want to be underfoot," I say.

"Not at all," he says. "Anna's crazy busy and so are my parents. I'm glad you can be here to share this day with me."

"Fantastic. Let's start this Kishinev adventure!"

I follow Leo half a block down the street, where we stop among a crowd of people clustered curbside at the base of a stanchion that supports overhead wires. Steel tram lines lead away in either direction.

An electric tram car—white on top and dark blue on the bottom—rolls up, powered by the overhead wires. Leo and I let those who were there before us board first, and in deference to an older couple vying for the last open seats, we stand for the ride, holding onto the overhead bars.

The tram hums up Stephan cel Mare Boulevard through a busy retail district and past an imposing, yellow-and-white, government building that has an arch over the main entrance.

"What's the plan?" I ask.

"Anna's family is doing most of the arrangements for the wedding and reception, so, I thought we could go to the *banya* and get clean for the wedding."

I give Leo a thumbs up. "Sounds perfect! Tell me about Anna."

"Her name's Anna Grinberg. Let's see… She's blonde. Gorgeous. Brilliant. Totally my type. We met last summer in Odesa. On the beach. And… well… we fell in love."

"Is she from Odesa?" I ask.

"No, Bolgrad, by the Black Sea near the tip of Ukraine," he says.

"Yeah. Papa has been there. Halfway between Odesa and Bucharest. It's a key point in the supply chain from Romania to Ukraine," I say.

"Exactly," Leo says.

"That must have presented some logistical challenges during your courtship. I mean, the fact that you live in Kishinev, and she lives in Bolgrad."

"Short-term. We both spent a lot of time on the train. Well, I went there mostly. I love it. You should go."

"I'd love to," I say, stopping myself from blurting out how I would kill to go just about anywhere.

"Anna has been here a few times. And we've met in in Odesa. But, uh, now she's moving here," Leo says.

"Fantastic," I say.

We pass more government buildings on the left.

Leo points at a domed structure built in a park to the right. "That's the Nativity Cathedral." The tram stops. Leo points again. "And that's our Triumphal Arch, built to commemorate some victory of the Russians over the Ottomans. I'm told it looks a lot like the Arc de Triomphe in Paris."

I don't respond, for fear of uttering something unworldly. We stand, disembark, and stroll up Alexander Pushkin Street to the sound of birds chirping.

"So how is it, living here in Kishinev?" I ask.

"Fine, fine. Business is going great," Leo says.

"Better than in Kalarash?"

"Oh, much. The furniture company is four times as big; I'm making way better money. I can get on the train, go to Odesa, bask on the beach…"

"But what about… the people?" I ask.

"Just before we moved here, the politics were a mess. In case you didn't hear in the shtetl, there was a revolution in Russia. In late 1917, Bessarabia elected its own parliament and proclaimed itself as the Moldavian Democratic Republic. The next January, Bolshevik troops occupied Kishinev, but the Romanian Army intervened… and ever since then we've been part of Romania."

"Yeah, we caught parts of that on the radio, and you may recall that we do have a paper," I say. "It's locals here who worry me. Isn't it scary?"

"Scary?" Leo asks, somewhat rhetorically.

"My whole life, Kishinev, the Christians, this city's aura—at least in papa's mind—hangs over my life like a treachery of ravens. Nobody talks about it, but what happened in 1903 casts a pall over everything we do. It darkens where we live, where we go, and with whom we associate. Papa will NEVER forget what happened, and therefore I can never leave the shtetl."

"The cloud still lingers."

"How many people did they kill?" I ask.

"About fifty. They wounded hundreds, plundered countless businesses, torched whole neighborhoods, and destroyed all sixty synagogues," Leo says.

"Any repercussions?"

"They created the illusion that they tried a few people, but they received light sentences."

"So, who's to blame? The Tsar?"

"He turned a blind eye."

"The mob of peasants?"

"They did it, but they were steered by politicians, police, heavily by the Russian Orthodox Church, and in a huge way by the media. You know, cultivated society. They instigated it and rejoiced over the murders."

"Including my brother and sister," I say.

"We could find their graves. The Jewish cemetery is right up the street."

"No, no, no. Not today. But that's why my—our—parents got on the train toward Kiev, rode two hours into the middle of nowhere, got off, and started over," I say.

"Yep," Leo says.

"It makes sense. We're close enough to survive and be sustained by the city," I say.

"But too far for recreational Jew killing," Leo says.

We walk in silence for an entire block.

"Now that you're back again, aren't you afraid?" I ask.

"Yes and no. I mean, do I fear for my life right now?" We both glance back at the cathedral. "No. There are now more than seventy synagogues here. Do Christians still hate Jews? Yes. Not all of them, but most of them. Pogroms have happened all over Europe since the Middle Ages. Anti-Semitism has been ingrained in who they are for centuries, and I don't think it will ever go away."

"Okay, let's talk about something pleasant," I say.

"Good idea," Leo says.

"Today is your wedding day! I'm so happy for you."

"Thank you. Thank you. How is your love life?" Leo asks.

"I said let's talk about something pleasant," I say.

We both laugh.

I add, "It's like my job here in Kishinev, working as a musician… I don't have one."

Leo and I get settled in at his parents' house, where I leave all my belongings, except for what I'll need at the *banya,* in his room.

"Anna and I have a suite at the hotel where the wedding will be," Leo says. "I'm pretty sure that's where they are now. You'll see them later."

We head back to where we got off the tram. After a short wait, we board it, pay our fair, and ride it to the Kishinev Banya off Armenian Street, three tram stops southeast of Stephan cel Mare.

As we disembark from the tram, I feast my eyes on women, lots of them, of all shapes, sizes, and ages, coming and going from their side of the banya, which, per usual, is on the front of the building. We go around back and enter on the men's side, chatting away about old times in Kalarash.

Carrying tote bags filled with clean clothes, our toilet kits and wool sauna hats, we stop just inside at the cashier's desk, where a man in his fifties glares at us from under wispy blonde bangs.

"I've got it," Leo insists, paying the man an entrance fee, at which time he hands us each a pair of towels.

We enter the locker room where, it being Saturday, it's busy, and men of all ages—from little boys to old grandpas—mill about in various degrees of undress. The room is humid and smells like mildew. I'm relieved that I don't see any bugs crawling around, and the floor appears to have been recently mopped.

Leo and I undress, stash our belongings in lockers, wrap one towel around our waists, drape the other over our shoulders and don our wool hats. We proceed to a tile-clad room where patrons lather themselves under a row of showerheads. A wooden door opens at the far end, where a furry Armenian emerges, ushered by a billow of steam. Across the room, a line of tables supports patrons enjoying massages.

As we hang our towels and hats on hooks, two adjacent showerheads become available, which we quickly commandeer, and we both crank on our showers. I shudder and let out a deep sigh as hot water pounds onto the back of my neck. As I scrub my hair and body, black coal ash from the train darkens the suds that, along with tension from my journey, run into the drain.

After showering, Leo directs me into the steam room where we slip on our wool hats to prevent our heads from overheating.

Next to the stove in the corner of the room, Leo manhandles a ladle protruding from a wooden bucket full of water.

An old man cracks a friendly smile and scoots over to make room on a wooden bench for them. About ten other men occupy two rows of benches, one higher than the other, that line the walls inside the room on three sides.

Leo scoops the ladle in the water and pours it on the stove, causing a tuft of steam to hiss as it curls into the air. Also soaking in the bucket are multiple *veniks*, bundles of birch branches, harvested during the summer when the trees are in flower and tied together to form something resembling crude brooms.

"Want to get flogged?" Leo asks.

"Sure," I whisper, as I spread out one of my towels and lie down on my stomach. I roll up the other and use it as a pillow.

Leo extracts a venik, waves it to direct the steam toward me and then begins swatting my back and legs, at first gently and then with increasing vigor. The other men chat softly and pay no attention as to our antics.

I convulse in pleasure, relishing the smell of the birch leaves, noticing how the sensation now is much different, bordering on erotic, compared to when papa similarly flogs me at the banya in Kalarash.

In time, we switch positions and I return the favor of flogging the groom to be. Swat, swat, swat, swat. In the moment, I enjoy being a percussionist.

Following a sufficient use of venik, we sit up next to each other and bask in the steam.

"You must be excited about tonight," I say.

"That's an understatement," Leo says.

"I'm envious. God, so envious. I don't even have a girlfriend," I say.

"You never know where you'll find one."

"Yeah. Who knows?

"Maybe tonight."

"Maybe."

We exchange glances and share a chuckle.

"But I have a stupid question," I say.

"What?"

I pick up a loose birch leave and smell it as I crush it in my fingers. "When you do fall in love… how do you know? I mean, I've never been in love."

"For me, I knew it the instant it happened," Leo says.

"Seriously?" I ask.

"Seriously," he says.

"How did you know? How did it happen?"

"I was just strolling on Langeron Beach in Odesa, toes in the sand, in truth, I was by myself on a lazy afternoon, looking for seashells. Out of nowhere, I looked up, and there she was, walking toward me. My heart started thumping against my chest, we made eye contact for one, two, three full seconds. We both smiled, and then we passed each other."

"And then?" I ask.

"I was like, oh my God, what just happened? I stopped, turned around and she did the same. I couldn't believe it. I took a deep breath, walked up to her, and said, 'Hi, my name is Leo.'"

"That was it?"

"That was it. We started talking… and we've never stopped."

"That's amazing."

"It was," Leo says.

"I'm jealous," I say.

We sit in silence for some time until we're both dripping with sweat. Leo raises his eyebrows and gestures his head toward the door. I agree, and we exit the steam room.

After a nice, long rinse under the showers, Leo says, "Now I have a surprise for you. I've arranged for us to get massages."

"I've never had one," I say.

"You're in for a treat."

"Isn't it expensive?"

"Papa's treat." Leo shrugs. "It's my wedding day."

Leo negotiates. We wait several minutes until two masseurs emerge and escort us to massage tables. I lie face-down on a massage table and close my eyes, as does he. At first it hurts, and I feel mildly violated as the masseur digs his thumbs and elbows into my back. I groan in pain and then in pleasure as he massages me from head to toe. The hour passes faster than any I've ever experienced.

We shower again, dress in the locker room, and regroup in a small cafe at the entrance to the banya, where a cup of tea warms us from the inside.

CHAPTER 3

I'm awestruck by the look of love and happiness on Leo's face when he says, "With this ring, you are made holy to me, for I love you as my soul. You are now my wife."

Tears well up in my eyes, and I attempt to hide my emotional reaction from the other attendees, yet I shake all over and I breathe in quick bursts as the words, "I love you as my soul," reverberate in my mind.

A band plays, and a group of girls holding hands take over the middle of the room, swaying their quaffed hair and pastel gowns to the beat of the music. I scrutinize each one. They're all attractive—most of them—but none yanks a gritty bow across my heart strings. Soon the whole wedding party, including me, is up and moving, everyone dancing with everyone.

After several songs, I take a breather, blotting the perspiration from my forehead. I make eye contact with the leader of the musicians. I had arrived early and we'd pre-meditated my performance for the evening. With black curly hair and a long nose, he looks like my mental image of Paganini. He raises his eyebrows. I gather myself, confidently step onto the stage, and grab my violin. The crowd goes quiet.

Though it wasn't pre-planned, Leo appears from the crowd. Leo clears his throat, and with Anna and the whole crowd watching, he says, "Thank you all everyone for coming tonight and sharing my wedding with Anna. I love you, Anna, and I just want to say that it's wonderful to see the coming together of these two families and sets of friends. I am so happy!"

The crowd cheers and applauds.

"Of course, I want to thank Anna's parents—and my parents—for making all this possible. And without further ado, I want to introduce a surprise guest, my best friend from Kalarash—Elazar Gershovich, who is going to play a song for us tonight. Elazar."

I take a deep breath, summon my most confident facial expression, and say, "Thank you, Leo. Congratulations to you and Anna. Feeling the love in this group tonight, I can tell yours is a very special and lasting bond. I wish you all the best."

The crowd applauds.

"In honor of tonight, I have prepared—and earlier co-conspired with your extraordinarily talented band—

to perform for you tonight *Serenade* by Franz Shubert, which was published a few months after his death. One of the last things he ever wrote, it's a short story of a person wishing to be loved by another."

I cradle my violin under my chin, glance at the band leader, and at his direction, we launch into Shubert's *Serenade*. I play with more heart and feeling than I ever have, and when I finish, the crowd erupts into cheers.

I raise my hand in thanks, bow, and swing my hand back to acknowledge the band. Then, without missing a beat, I set my violin on its stand, exit the stage, and the band launches into another song.

Leo, who's surrounded by a group of family members, looks over and gives me a thumbs up. I smile, nod my head, then look across the room to where a circle of young women ladling a pinkish liquid into cups from a punch bowl captures my attention.

Suddenly, my heart misses a beat when I see… the woman of my dreams? Could it be? I can only see her chiseled features, pronounced eyelashes, stylish clothing. Hmm. Maybe she could be *the one*.

I fear she'll slip away in the other direction, but then, as if by the will of God, she pivots her head in my direction and our eyes lock… one, two, three… our souls fuse… one, two, three… we smile… mutual surprise radiates… and then a group of dancers obscures our line of vision.

My breathing shallows and my heart palpitates as I push and shove my way toward the punch bowl, to where I beheld this vision of loveliness, but when I get there, she is gone.

The band switches to a bouncier tune, and the whole wedding party gravitates onto the dance floor and moves to the beat.

I see her again, this time full-frontal, then pirouetting as she laughs and dances with a troupe of her female friends. She has a swan's confident movements, and she is *hot*. Searing hot. She wears a green, knee-length dress that has long sleeves, a V-neck accented by a bow perched upon her bosom, and a flowing belt that ties on her left hip. White high heels elevate her stature, and her wavy-brown hair is cut short above her shoulders.

She sees me, grins girlishly, and I dance over to her, this time maintaining eye contact.

With a graceful twirl, she splits from her cohorts and at once we are one, dancing together, our bodies instantly in sync. I extend my hands. She grasps them, and in perfect rhythm with the music I twirl her to the right and then to the left. We both radiate positive energy. I set her free and she closes her eyes, yet returns, moving in unison with my soul. She takes my hands and spins me. I spin her back and our rhythmic link intensifies as the song reaches its crescendo. Then, as it ends, I reel her into an embrace as her essence of perfume and perspiration fills my nose.

I gently release her, push my glasses up on my nose, and take in her stationary vision. "Hi. I'm Elazar," I say as we exit the dance floor toward the punch bowl. Her ethereal quality takes my breath away like a fairytale character come to life—a princess transformed into a real girl. Part of me believed that she existed only in my imagination.

"I'm Ita."

I struggle to hear her over the music. "EEE-tuh? Ita."

"Yes."

"What a beautiful name. It's so nice to meet you."

"Likewise," she says.

Now that I have a chance to look at her, up close, I try to put the pieces together. How to reconcile the angelic voice, the curvy physique, the lightness of her persona in my dreams with this sleek, classy goddess in front of me?

"You can really move," she says.

"So can you! No choreographer necessary," I say.

She starts to say something else, I suspect related to my performance, when the band starts playing another song, thus limiting our ability to converse. I'm tempted to swoop her back onto the dance floor, but the cluster of girls Ita was dancing with—before I commandeered her—also return from the dance floor, visibly sizing me up.

"Oh, I'd like you to meet my friends," Ita says.

"I'd be delighted," I say.

"This is Tsilia, Sofia and Raisa. Ladies, this is Elazar."

"Hello," they all say.

"You're amazing on the violin," Tsilia says.

"Isn't he?" Ita exclaims.

I blush as they all profusely agree.

"I love the sentiment that it is about a person wishing to be loved," Ita says. "You can feel two different things: melancholy yearning and hope. They shift back and forth, back, and forth."

"That's very astute of you," I say as our eyes connect. "I do believe that was Shubert's intent." Our eye contact lingers.

"And wasn't that a lovely ceremony?" Tsilia asks, severing our eye bond.

"Very moving," I say.

As I take command and fill each of us a glass from the punch bowl, Ita says, "When Anna's father led her to the chuppah… Goosebumps!"

"The blessings…" Raisa says.

"Everything," Sofia says.

I raise my glass and, looking into Ita's eyes, I say, "Here's to joy, happiness and marital bliss."

"Cheers!" they all say as we clink glasses and sip.

"Are you a friend of the bride or the groom?" I ask Ita.

"The bride. We've been best friends since grade school. How about you?"

"The groom. We're cousins." I conduct with my index finger. "His papa is my mama's brother. Our papas have done business with one another."

There's a pause in the conversation. Ita's friends exchange glances with each other, and Raisa says, "We're going to go look at the fountain in the entryway and let you two have a chat."

"Okay, thanks," Ita says, waving good-bye with her fingers.

"Nice meeting you," I say, and as they fade into the crowd, I add, "Do you want to find someplace quieter where we can sit down?"

"Sure."

I follow Ita away from the band, and we find an unoccupied bench on a patio outside and take a seat next to each other.

Now it's a little awkward. I'm not worried, though. I'm so energized by the moment, it's like I'm hovering on a cloud. We're sitting side by side, and in the silence, I'm wondering if there is anything stuck between my front teeth. It's a warm summer evening and I'm aware that we are both sweating from dancing.

"So where are you from?" she asks, and I say, at the same time, "So, you must be from Bolgrad."

"Yes. That's where Anna and I went to school together."

"Tell me about it," I say. "I want to know everything about you, and how you ended up here, tonight, at this wedding."

She raises her eyebrows, seemingly amused. She tells me about how Bolgrad is a beautiful place near the Prut/ Danube Delta, close to a lagoon on the Black Sea. She mentions that being part of Romania, it has loose tax laws, and is a good place to do business. That many Jews moved there to distance themselves from Russians. How her family owns a chain of stores that sell fabric and home furnishings. That they have a big house in the center of town with a housekeeper, and basically that she's well-to-do.

I'm listening closely, but only catching every other word. Instead, I'm noticing how her dress is exquisitely stitched, of the highest-quality fabric and tailored perfectly to emphasize her breasts, and that her arms are perfectly tanned. I look into her eyes, sparkling and blue. She delicately sips her punch between words, and I watch her long neck contract as she swallows.

Women like this, I think, *do not exist in Kalarash.*

"What do you do? Or what do you want to do with your life?" I ask.

"What do you do?" she counters.

"I'm in business," I say. "I work for my papa. My parents own a hardware and tack store, you know… where we sell everything from tools and building supplies to saddles, bridles, and halters…" I stop. My mind goes blank. She wants to know more.

"So… is the store here in Kishinev?"

"No. In Kalarash."

"Right," she says.

"The shtetl. A couple of hours northwest of here." I point over my shoulder with my thumb.

"Oh, yes," she says, then opens her mouth to say something else, but closes it. She blinks multiple times, and I can tell that something, something not entirely favorable as far as I'm concerned, is running through her mind.

The band starts playing an upbeat dance song, and I take Ita by the hand and in a flash we're back inside, dancing like Gypsies for what seems like hours and then slow dancing for the rest of time.

At a break in the music, we encounter the bride and groom. We all have a nice chat about the wedding and the guests and the decorations, how fabulous the bride looks, some other female friends of Anna's appear and the noise level in the room goes through the roof as the women squeal with their high-pitched voices and celebrate. At the same time I congratulate Leo and meet some of his other male friends, all the while not being able to quit thinking about Ita. I look over, we make eye contact, and after what seems to me as way too long, we re-connect.

We go back outside to our private bench, and we talk more about Shubert, the violin, how my family is a musical ensemble, and silly stories about Herschel and my new nephew. I describe the vineyards in Kalarash—now closed by the Romanian prohibition—and the exquisite wine and cognac. She wants to know all about living in the shtetl—the rabbis, the synagogues, the holidays—and I find that I'm surprised at the truths and mistruths in the stereotypes. After a while, I'm not sure if she's genuinely interested or just nodding along out of politeness. Or something else.

"What do you do?" I finally ask.

"I'm an artist," she says.

"Wow," I say, shocked, maybe even a bit dubious, but impressed. "What kind of artist?"

"I paint. Mostly oil on canvas, but I also have a penchant for watercolors."

"I'd love to see your work. Do you do… portraits?"

"Landscapes."

"Really? Why landscapes?"

"It's a long story."

"I want to hear it."

"I started very young. When I was eight, I spent the summer in Paris."

"No way. You've been to Paris?"

"Yes. Our whole family went; all eight of us. My great-great grandfather was from there. We've been several times, but the first time, I had an amazing art teacher who put a brush in my hand and encouraged me to paint… and I just, gravitated toward landscapes."

"Paris?"

"*Oui. Je parle francais. Le faites vous?*"

"Excuse me?"

"I speak French. Do you?"

"Uh… No."

She gives me a mischievous smile, I think, or is it condescending? "Paris is unbelievable. When I'm there, I live, speak and breath French Culture. I soak up knowledge about food, art, history, geography…"

"Do you do touristy things?"

"Of course. I've been up in the Eiffel Tower, toured the catacombs… taken boat rides on the Seine."

My mind wanders as I imagine myself with her on a boat on the river in Paris, whatever it's called.

"Have you done much traveling?" she asks.

"Not really," I say out loud, thinking about how I've never been anywhere.

She continues as if she didn't hear me. She says, "Most importantly, I have continued taking private art lessons from an amazing woman named Marianne. She has taught me so much about color and brush technique. Early on, I was working on a landscape… of the Alps near Vienna. She told me, at that age, that my work 'contains a spark of the Divine.' I believed her."

"I love it. So, you studied art through high school?"

"Yes. And I've been accepted to the Bolgrad College of Art. I begin a four-year program in September."

"I see."

"When I graduate, I'm moving to Paris."

We look into each other's eyes for what, to me, seems like an eternity.

"Three of my sisters live there." She looks away.

My mind reels. I think of my dreams of being a musician and moving a mere fifty kilometers to Kishinev…

"Are you Jewish?" I ask.

"Yes," she says, a bit offended.

"Are your parents going to move when you do?"

"No."

"How did your sisters manage to move there? What do they do?"

I've clearly exceeded her willingness to respond to my interrogation when, fortunately, the band starts playing an up-beat folk song. I change the subject, "Another dance?"

We dance some more. We exchange more small talk. Finally, the evening is coming to an end, and my mind is reeling about how we can connect this moment to the rest of our lives. "What are you doing tomorrow? I'd love to see you again before I go back to Kalarash."

She takes a deep breath, then gives me a sad, almost pathetic look. Shaking her head, she says. "I have to catch an eight o'clock train in the morning."

"Can we keep in touch?"

"Yeah, sure," she says, with hesitance.

"Will you give me your address?" I ask, trying not to sound desperate, and before she can respond, I produce a pencil and a piece of paper and hand it to her. "I'll write."

She takes a deep breath, smiles, and takes the pencil and paper. She leans over a nearby table, and, in exquisite handwriting, writes her name and address on the paper.

She rights herself, turns, and hands me the paper and pen. "It was nice meeting you."

"It was nice meeting you!" I say, and I spread my arms, hoping for a hug and a kiss.

She gives me a quick peck on the cheek and says, "Have a nice life in Kalarash."

"I promise I'll write! Maybe I'll come visit you in Bolgrad."

"We'll see," she says, waving with her fingers, and, like a swan from a wetland, she flies away.

CHAPTER 4

6 August, 1922, 07:15 — The next morning, my eyes open. I'm naked and alone in Leo's bed, and all I can think about is Ita. I smell of her perfume, her perspiration, her essence. I can taste her neck. I look at my watch and calculate that in 45 minutes, her train will leave for Bolgrad.

I may never see her again. I. Can't. Let. That. Happen.

I jump out of bed, dress, and run downstairs, where I'm relieved to see that Leo's parents are still sleeping. I chug a glass of water, hurry out back and use the outhouse, wash my hands and face, and contemplate running on foot all the way to the train station. I know I'll never make it in time, so I sprint toward the tram.

With God on my side, a tram car rolls up just as I get to the stop, and it's headed in the right direction. Breathing hard, I climb on, pay my fare, and then will with all my might that the tram makes it to the train station in time. With each stop, I resist screaming at old people to hurry up as they board.

As the tram approaches the stop at the train station, I crowd my way to the door. The minute the car stops and the door opens, I leap off, sprint across the street, nearly get run over by a horse and buggy, and, as if in a dream, I fly toward the station.

It's a busy morning, and lots of people are arriving to catch trains. Frantically, I scan the crowd, hoping, praying. Please God, let me see her. One. More. Time.

Suddenly, there she is, perched on the main platform of the Kishinev Central Train Station, dressed in blue and standing next to a middle-aged woman wearing a big hat adorned with a pink-satin cabbage rose. Her train is already there, and she is hugging the woman good-bye.

"Ita! Ita!" I yell as I approach.

Both women turn and when Ita recognizes me, she says, "Elazar?"

My heart leaps at the sound of her vocalizing my name and I approach them trying to catch my breath.

"Oh, Ita," I say.

"What are you doing here?"

"I couldn't bear to let you leave without saying goodbye. One more time."

"Isn't that sweet!" says the woman with Ita. "Who is this?"

"The guy I met last night," Ita says. "Elazar, this is my Aunt Rosa. Aunt Rosa, this is Elazar."

"Hello. Elazar Gershovich," I say, kissing Rosa's hand. I already feel like she is my aunt.

"Hello." She smiles approvingly.

"Good looks obviously run in the family," I say.

Rosa blushes. "That's so nice of you to say."

I turn to Ita, take her by the hands, and say, "I'm so glad I caught you. I thought about you all night." I close my eyes and take a deep breath. "I just want you to know that I've never met anyone I felt so attracted to. So connected to. You are my dream."

"Oh, Lazar."

"Is it possible that we could see each other again?"

"Yes."

"Oh! That makes me so happy."

She kisses me, this time on the lips.

"All aboard!" a conductor announces.

"Unfortunately, right now, I have to get on the train," Ita says.

I kiss her back, just enough, and I feel real chemistry, like when we were dancing. "Of course. Don't miss your train."

Ita hugs her aunt. "Goodbye."

Aunt Rosa waves. "Goodbye."

Ita picks up her suitcase and says, "Goodbye. It really was great meeting you."

"See you soon. I'll write. I'll come to Bolgrad. I promise."

CHAPTER 5

7 August, 1922 — As I unpack my suitcase in my bedroom following an afternoon train ride back to pathetic Kalarash, I bury my face in the suit I wore to the wedding and inhale Ita. I may never wash my suit.

Go to the wedding; weddings are great places to meet girls, mama says. Right. Did it happen? Maybe. Did I really meet someone nice, who would want to have a relationship with… with me? 'Twere if it were so. She talked to me, we danced all night, she gave me her address. Then again, I shouldn't get my hopes up too much; she's out of my league, her papa's rich, not some shopkeeper from the shtetl. But oh, she's so… exquisite. When she smiles and looks into my eyes, I want to melt.

"Elazar! Dinner is ready," mama calls from the kitchen.

"I'll be right there," I call down the stairs. I finish unpacking, cram my suitcase under my bed and in a daze, and amble down the stairs one step at a time into the kitchen, collapsing into a chair at the breakfast table. Herschel and Sarah are at her parents' house, and papa's working late in the store. It's just the two of us, and mama does something she has never done. I was fourteen when prohibition started. She uncorks a bottle of wine, pours two glasses, and puts one in front of me. "How was the wedding?"

Mama and I have a special bond. Maybe it had something to do with what happened during the pogrom, or maybe it was straight out of the womb, I don't know, but our house has always been divided into two camps: Papa and Herschel in one, and mama and I in the other.

I take a glug of wine and say, "It was unbelievable!" An image of Ita comes into my mind. "Anna and Leo looked so happy. Everything went perfectly."

She takes a sip, and says, "Perfectly?"

"Yeah."

"Give me some details. What else happened?"

"Nothing," I lie.

"You met someone, didn't you?" Mama puts a loaf of braided *challah* bread between us.

"Maybe."

"Maybe?"

"Okay, yes, but I'm trying not to let myself get too excited," I say, breaking off a piece of challah and stuffing it into my mouth.

"Why? Come on."

I chew, thinking, and swallow. I wash it down with another sip of wine. "It's a longshot."

"What's her name?"

"Ita. Ita Kaplan."

"Hmm."

"Yes. A nice, Jewish girl."

"What does she look like?" mama asks as she goes to the stove and ladles two bowls of *cholent*, a slow-cook soup made from meats, grains, and beans, and serves it cold with leftovers from the night before. She puts a bowl in front of me and one in her place.

I sniff the soup. It's usually not my favorite, but tonight it smells delicious. "She has brown wavy hair, blue eyes, and a body like a goddess."

"How did you meet?" Mama sits and takes a bite of *cholent*.

I tell her about how we met on the dance floor with lots of details about her hair, her dress, how we talked, where she's from, how she's out of my league, wants to be an artist, is going to art school in the fall then moving to Paris.

Mama sips her wine. "So, that's it?"

"I don't want to be the one who kills her dream."

"So, you just said goodbye and now you'll never see her again?"

"Not exactly." I tell her about seeing Ita off at the train station. "And she gave me her address."

"Have you composed a letter?"

"All the way home on the train. But that's another problem. It's almost the middle of August. If I send her a letter suggesting that I come see her, by the time it gets to Bolgrad, and then she responds, assuming she does so right away, by the time I get the response and we negotiate a time for me to come see her, it's going to be well into September and she'll be busy with school."

Mama takes a sip of wine. "Looks to me like you have two choices. Marry Klara Brantman—"

I cringe.

"—or go to Bolgrad and show this Ita Kaplan that you want to spend the rest of your life with her."

CHAPTER 6

19 August, 1922, 08:00 — Less than two weeks after Leo's wedding, Kalarash is already heating up as I board a train bound for Bolgrad, carrying my rucksack, a bedroll, my violin, and a determined countenance. It's Saturday morning. Papa made me work yesterday, then last night was Shabbat, so I stayed home for the family dinner. Today, I should be enjoying a day of rest but we're not as orthodox as some people, so today, papa is letting me go in search of my dreams.

Two hours into the southbound journey I blot my brow with a handkerchief as the train bends along with the Bic River—a polluted drainage ditch—past the domes of the Nativity Cathedral in the distance and stops where it has since trains were first built, in the southeast corner of Kishinev. On the platform, in my imagination, I can almost see Ita as she was, so beautiful, only a few weeks before.

It gets hotter and more humid as the train continues south. My armpits and crotch get sweatier with every stop. I doze as endless fields of wheat, sunflowers, and rye speed by. I try to convince myself how lucky I am that I'm not traveling on foot or on a horse. That used to take a week or more, but it's a really long train ride, and the bench I'm sitting on seems to get more ridged by the hour.

After a sixteen-hour journey, with the train going southeast for about eight hours, almost to Odesa, before it turned southwest toward Bolgrad, my train pulls into a station that looks like it was built in the late 1800s, smack in the middle of Bolgrad.

It's midnight. The train's destination is Bucharest, so I'm one of only a handful to get off. The others quickly disperse, and I am soon the only person there. Rucksack over my shoulder, violin case in hand, I cross the street to a park, where I find a level patch of grass under a tree, roll out my bedroll and camp for the night.

I'm wide awake and nobody is around, so I take out my violin and quietly peruse my repertoire. Like always, it soothes my inner being. Maybe half an hour later, my head nods and I yawn, so I put away my violin and tuck myself into my bedroll.

All night, I dream about Ita—wild, passionate dreams, dreams I'd be ashamed to tell my mama.

CHAPTER 7

20 August, 1922 — I wake the next morning as the park comes to life with train travelers, dust myself off and assemble my belongings. Mama equipped me well, and thusly, I swig water from my canteen, chomp an apple, savor a bread roll, and then freshen up in the men's room in the train station.

A few meters down the platform, I approach a uniformed conductor and hand him a piece of paper. In my best Romanian, I say, "Excuse me, will you please give me directions to this address?"

I pay close attention as the conductor points and gesticulates and then proceed as directed.

I walk fifteen or so blocks through an upscale neighborhood lined with birch and linden trees until I find the address Ita wrote in loopy handwriting a few weeks earlier.

When my brain connects the address to the vision before me, I feel like a peasant and almost turn around and run all the way back to Kalarash. There, in majestic splendor, stands a white, two-story mansion, fronted with Ionic columns.

I look at the address again and I envision myself, with my rucksack in the clothes I wear, and I feel… insufficient. Who am I kidding? I met this woman once, okay, and I sprinted to the train station and said goodbye, and even met her aunt. Now I show up to this mansion early on a Sunday morning, unannounced, and expect her to welcome me with open arms? Pathetic.

I turn around and start walking back toward the train station. I spend the better part of the day wandering around Bolgrad, familiarizing myself with the downtown area, trying to decide what I am going to do. After lunch, I find a park and spend a couple of hours practicing my violin, going through my repertoire.

I remind myself that this could be a day that makes or breaks my life. A melody surges into my head, musically expressing the sentiments of a person wishing to be loved by another. Now that it's a more civilized hour, as if guided by an otherworldly power, I turn and walk back to the base of the stairs of the Kaplan house that lead up to her porch. I drop my rucksack, kneel, open my violin case, and extract my violin and bow.

I stand, gather myself, place the wooden instrument beneath my chin and with a quiet series of plucks, strokes and turns of the tuning pegs, I refine its tune. I take a deep breath, close my eyes, and… dah, da da dah… commence playing Franz Shubert's *Serenade*.

I advance to maybe a quarter of the way into the piece when the door opens. I'm puzzled when a middle-aged woman—a Gypsy wearing a black dress and a white apron—peers out through deep brown eyes. I smile and pour even more feeling into my interpretation.

Midway through, an older, impeccably dressed woman, quite possibly of French high society, joins the Gypsy at the door and they sway to the rhythm of my violin. Doubt infiltrates my countenance that perhaps I'm in the wrong place. But then, like a vision from the depths of my dreams, Ita materializes even more lovely than I remember, and I know that she knows, it's me as I pour my soul into the final third of the serenade.

The three women stand, clearly enraptured by my performance, and behind their hands whisper to one another. I smell the essence of French perfume as Ita slowly descends the staircase. I finish the final measures, and after the last note, the three applaud.

I take off my hat and bow as if to a house full of royalty.

"Oh my God, Elazar," Ita says as she closes the gap between us, embraces me and gives me a kiss. She's even more svelte than I remember, dressed in a white, short-sleeved sweater with narrow blue stripes across her chest that is tucked into high-waisted trousers with cuffs dangling above white high-heeled shoes. My soul melts.

"I can't believe you're here," she says.

"I promised I would come."

"So soon. It's only been what? Two weeks."

"It seems like forever to me."

"You said you'd write." I can tell she's a bit taken aback.

"That would have taken weeks. I want to see you again before school started… so I'd be less of an intrusion," I say.

Ita turns around. "Mama."

"Who have we here?" Ita's mama says, arms folded, wearing a long-sleeved black sweater, a white, shin-length skirt with a scalloped hem, black nylons and while heels not unlike Ita's, but fastened with an ankle strap. "Are you going to introduce me?"

"This is Elazar Gershovich, the violinist I met at Anna's wedding. Elazar, this is my mama, Charna Kaplan."

"Well, well, well. Hello, Elazar. That was some performance."

"Thank you…"

"Charna. You may call me Charna."

"Hello, Charna," I say as I shake her hand and look into her brown eyes.

"Oh, and this is Anica, our housekeeper," Ita says gesturing to the woman who first opened the door.

Anica smiles.

"Well, come in," Charna says.

Ita blushes, beckons me, and smiles. "Come in, come in."

She watches as I put away my violin, pick up my rucksack, and ascend the stairs.

I feel underdressed like a peasant as I step into a two-story atrium with beige tile floors and follow the women into a cavernous living room. On the far side is a dining table that would seat forty people and beyond, I see into a spacious kitchen. Charna leads me to an overstuffed leather couch.

"Have a seat," she says.

"That's very kind of you," I say as I take off my rucksack, awkwardly set it on the floor and sit down.

Charna clasps her hands. "You must be parched. Would you like some refreshment? Water? Tea? Lemonade?"

"Yes, please," I say. "Um, lemonade would be wonderful."

"I'll have the same, please," Ita says.

"Anica," Charna calls to the housekeeper, "would you get us three lemonades, please."

The housekeeper acknowledges and disappears.

"I could have sent a telegram," I say. "I guess we still live in ancient times in Kalarash. Please forgive me for showing up like this," I say.

"I must admit, it is a surprise," Ita says.

"I just had to see you."

"It's a busy weekend. School starts next week…"

Charna interrupts. "How long are you here?"

"Until Tuesday."

There was an awkward silence.

"I have a place where I stay," I lie, avoiding glancing at the bedroll clipped to my rucksack.

"Don't be silly; you can stay here. We have four empty bedrooms."

"I don't want to impose."

"Not at all," Charna insists. "Two nights. Do you have other plans?" Charna asks Ita.

"No," Ita says. "There's just a lot bouncing around in my head. It's good to see you, Lazar. This is going to be fun." Ita forces a smile.

The housekeeper enters carrying a tray with three glasses of lemonade. Charna stands and like the grand hostess that she is, hands the first one to me. I stand and accept it. She gives the second to Ita and keeps the third for herself.

I raise my glass and say, "It's a pleasure to be here, it's an honor to meet you Charna, and words cannot express how happy I am to see you, Ita."

As we all sip our lemonade, I scan the room and my eyes land on a painting on the wall next to the dining-room table. It's a landscape.

Rising and walking toward it, almost involuntarily, I say, "Is this one of your paintings?"

"Oh, that? Yes. That's one of my earlier pieces," Ita says.

The painting depicts springtime in the mountains—I'm guessing the Carpathians—with sunbathed spruce trees in the foreground painted in whites and pinks. Behind the spruce trees are brown foothills leading to increasingly jagged peaks done in shades of purple, fading to blue and silhouetted by an orangish, cloudy sky.

"It's magnificent. You really do have a touch of the divine," I say.

"That's… what my teacher says."

"In Paris," I say. "I remember every word you told me that night at Leo's wedding."

"Every word?" Charna teases.

"Maybe not *every* word, but Ita wasn't exaggerating about her talent." I take a sip of my lemonade and savor it's sweet-and-sour flavor as I stare at the painting for what seems like forever.

Ita joins me before the work and watches me as I absorb the composition, the brush strokes, the highlights, the shadowing. "I'd love to see more paintings of yours," I say feeling as if I'm returning from a dreamworld.

"Of course," Charna says. "Go on, Ita. Show him your studio."

Ita leads me into the kitchen, which I'm impressed to see is double-kosher, or two kitchens in one room with separate sinks, dishes, flatware, and everything so that dairy and meat can be kept separate. Beyond the kitchen is a room that might have been a guest room or quarters for live-in help. Now it's Ita's realm.

There's an easel in the far corner supporting a work in progress. Next to it is a table cluttered with paint cans, tubes, and cups loaded with brushes of all shapes and sizes. Covering the walls and in stacks covering the baseboards are landscapes, still-lifes, and even a few portraits in varying degrees of completion—Ita's body of work.

Ita gives me a guided tour, narrating the subject of each painting, what period of her life it came from, what she was trying to accomplish, and artists, techniques, and historical periods from which she gained inspiration. I'm absorbed by her commentary, but the longer she talks, the more a sort of sadness and distance creeps into her demeanor.

I have some idea what's going through her head, so when its polite, I steer us back to the living room, to more chatting with Charna and she cheers up as my stay progresses.

Charna cooks us a wonderful dinner of sturgeon from the Black Sea. The three of us sit up, talking and laughing. I tell Charna—and fill in a lot of details—about my family and my life in Kalarash.

After a pause in the conversation, out pops a question that's been batting around in my head since I arrived. "Where is your papa? Away on business?"

"He, uh," Ita pauses, searching for the right phrase.

"He passed away," Charna says.

"I'm sorry. I… didn't know."

"Five years ago, this summer," Ita says.

"Oh, God. That must have been horrible."

"It was unexpected," Charna says. "And yes, we're still coming to terms with it."

"I still miss him every day," Ita says.

I take Ita's hand. Ita gives me a sad smile and squeezes my hand back.

In the course of the evening, details trickle out about how Ita's papa, Ira Kaplan, owned a chain of home improvement and fabric stores called *Parper Branner,* with branches in Moscow, Kiev, Warsaw, Kishinev, Bucharest, Odesa and Bolgrad. How on that fateful night in Odesa, papa ordered crab for dinner—not kosher— and suddenly couldn't breathe, turned colors, and died. How the former sales director, Vladimir Kovalenko now runs the business, and how they still have a comfortable income, and own an apartment in Odesa, an apartment building, and their house in Bolgrad.

I'm listening closely to every detail. Yes, I'm also noticing how much Ita resembles Charna, and I imagine how in twenty years she will look a lot like Charna… I could grow old with her.

When at last the candles drip onto the coffee table, the Kaplan women show me to one of their empty rooms, which the housekeeper graciously freshened for me earlier in the day. The bedspread is turned down, and there is water on the nightstand.

"Sweet dreams," Charna says.

I look longingly into Ita's eyes. She smiles, blows me a kiss, and closes the door.

I undress, snuggle into the feathery mass erected in a space that makes my bedroom at home seem like a miserable hovel. It's decorated in shades of pink with floral curtains, tasteful paintings adorning the walls—not Ita's work—and an exquisite oak desk, obviously the room of one of her sisters who moved to Paris.

I stare at the ceiling and imagine Ita in her bed only doors away. In my mind, I tip-toe down the hall, slip into her room and crawl into bed next to her, where she greets me with open arms, and we make mad, passionate love all night. Moments, maybe hours later, my mind shifts, and I envision myself creeping down the hall, and as I open Ita's door, smash my toe on a doorstop, cry out in pain and Ita shrieks in outrage at my violation of her space, I cower in shame as Charna rescues her daughter and I'm thrown out in the street. At last, I contain my passions with my arms folded atop the bedspread and fall into a restless sleep riddled with dreams, again, about a blissful life with Ita.

CHAPTER 8

21 August, 1922 — The next morning, Ita packs a picnic lunch, and we go on a scenic walk through Bolgrad.

"Many nationalities live here," she says, "including Bulgarians, Albanians, Gagauz, Russians, and Ukrainians, and each diaspora has retained its identity, traditions, and national cuisine."

She guides me through a park in the southeast corner of Bolgrad to a grassy knoll on the bank of a lagoon that connects to the Danube Delta and, beyond that, the Black Sea. We sit on a blanket, eat lunch, and she tells me more about *Parper Branner*, her family's fabric and furniture business, as we lounge in the warm summer sun.

After lunch, Ita sits with her legs crossed and I rest my head in her lap. She gently brushes my hair out of my face with her soft fingers and talks about her immediate family. I tune in and out as Ita tells me she's the fifth of six children, five girls and one boy, Solomon, who was the youngest but died at age five. How her next older sister, Riva, is married to Rachman Rabinovich, has a baby son, and they still live in Bolgrad, and how her three oldest sisters—Fania, Tanya and Alya—moved to Paris, attended Sorbonne University, and are starting a pharmaceutical company.

At this, I say, "I'm still confused. How did your family end up in Bolgrad? And get to…"

"Where we are in society?" she asks.

"Yes."

"It's a long story," she says.

"I want to hear it," I insist.

"My great grandfather, Lewis Kaplan grew up in the silk industry in Lyon, France. That's how far back we go in the fabric industry. Anyway, in 1853, at age nineteen, Lewis was drafted into the French army and shipped to fight in the Crimean War."

"What was that war about?" I ask.

"As I understand it, it was over Russia's rights to intervene in the affairs of Orthodox Christians living in Palestine, which was then Ottoman territory. France and Britain entered in March 1854, after the Russian-Ottoman conflict had clearly turned in Russia's favor," Ita says.

"It never ends, does it?" I say.

"This prolonged conflict, in which as many as one million people died, witnessed novel weaponry such as rockets, new forms of logistics, and communication via steamship, rail and telegraph, a fresh organization of military medicine with organized female nursing, and new forms of military journalism, including some photography."

"Seriously?" I ask.

Nodding, Ita continues: "Papa said the Crimean War served as a major watershed in modern world history and resulted in a great increase of British and French influence in the Middle East… And it was during that time that Great Grandpa Lewis met my great grandmother here in Bolgrad. Because of its strategic location—and a lot of other factors—they decided to stay."

"That's amazing," I say.

"In 1854, Gilles Kaplan, my grandfather, was born here. During that time, much change was being implemented by Napoleon III, including construction of the Suez Canal, establishment of Moldavia and Wallachia—later united to form Romania—and, in 1860, the Cobden-Chevalier Free Trade Agreement, which greatly expanded trade in Europe and granted many rights, including the right for women to be admitted to a French university."

"Wow! That's one of the reasons your sisters were able to go to Paris and attend Sorbonne University," I say.

"You have been listening," she says, winking, and continues, "While all that was happening, with funding and connections from his father, Lewis started *Parper Branner*—our fabric and later home furnishings company—here in Bolgrad in 1854. In the ensuing years, he groomed my grandfather, Gilles, to take over the family business. By then, the business was burgeoning, and in 1873, Grandpa Gilles married my grandmother. In 1874, my father Ira was born. And, well, here we are."

I look up into her eyes. "I could spend the rest of time listening to you talk about anything. I love to watch your lips. Every time they form a syllable your spell over me deepens."

Ita looks troubled. Me and my effusive mouth.

I change the subject to the weather, and we spend the rest of the afternoon watching the clouds float by, scoops of pelicans gliding over the shallow waters, and waves rippling up on the bank of the lagoon.

We walk back to Ita's house mostly in silence. I know what's going through her head.

We spend the evening enjoying a meal with Charna. Nobody says it, but all three of us feel that the magic has left the air… but my train doesn't leave until morning. I'm tempted to grab my rucksack and go camp near the train station. I know they know it's crossing my mind, but no one wants to be rude, I've already dirtied the sheets in the guest room, so we all do our best to enjoy the moment.

I retire to the guest room, and after much tossing and turning, I have a nightmare that we're together in a far-off place. We have two children, and we're all covered with insects. I awake in a pool of sweat.

22 August, 1922 — Charna is up early the next morning and fixes me tea and kasha for breakfast. When it's time for me to go catch my train, she bids me a polite good-bye and leaves Ita and I to ourselves.

"I shouldn't have come," I say as I face her and take her hands. "I know you are in school. There's no way I will stand in the way of your education… your dreams."

Ita looks even more troubled. "I am so selfish!"

"No," I say, "I'm selfish. I'm a peasant from the shtetl. I'm not good enough for you. A future with me wouldn't be… in Paris."

Tears run down Ita's face. "You're a handsome man… a nice guy… I'm not sorry you came… Right this minute, I don't want you to leave. But you're right, my heart says you shouldn't have come. I need to go to school, move to Paris and become an artist. I'm not going to let go of my dream."

"I wish you all the best."

"Thank you. The same to you."

"Well… I guess this is it," I say. "Fly my feathery friend into the pure field. Fly my beloved bird into the free space."

CHAPTER 9

3 October, 1922 – With the onset of Autumn, gloomy days, bitter cold, and the imminent approach of winter, my disposition descends into low notes I've never scratched before. When I'm not moving rocks or restacking lumber, or splitting firewood for the winter, I spend endless hours in my room, alone, playing my violin, delving into the gloomiest melodies of Strauss, Beethoven, and Haydn.

It's Tuesday. I'm taking inventory, wishing I could push away my loneliness and grief, when I hear the clop, clop of a horse-and-buggy arriving at the store. I emerge from behind a pile of railroad ties to see a crusty Georgian named David Gabashvili climb down from the driver's seat.

Old-man Gabashvili owns what used to be Kalarash's largest vineyard on the eastern outskirts of the shtetl. Now a tobacco/vegetable farm/orchard, for many years Gabashvili has been one of our best customers, yet deep down, papa, for lack of a better word, *hates* him and, by association, so do I. As groomed, I mentally prepare to double or triple the price of whatever he wants to buy.

I wave and say, "Hello!"

Sporting a bushy, salt-and-pepper mustache, he descends from the driver's seat of the buggy wearing a black suit, overcoat, leather boots and black chapeau. He fits his whip on its hook and says, "Good afternoon. Is Toiva in?"

"No, he and Herschel went into town. What can I do you for?"

"I need some building materials," he says.

He lights his pipe and puffs away as I escort him into the lumberyard. It turns out he wants our entire supply of wooden planks and studs, an ample stock of nails, and various tools. I keep a list on an invoice as he helps me load the supplies onto his buggy while he explains to me that his farm is doing very well, demand for his produce is up along with its prices, and he's expanding his barn in anticipation of it being even better in the spring.

Inside the store, I ring him up with the gouged prices and he happily pays.

Just as old-man Gabashvili's pulling out of our driveway, he pauses as a young woman approaches on foot from the direction of town.

I squint, push my glasses up on the bridge of my nose and, holy Moses, I don't know if it's by coincidence, or if they had planned on meeting here after she ran some other errand, but there, on Strada Alexandru cel Bun, is his daughter, Mariam, whom I haven't seen in quite some time. I see that she has… matured.

Wow. What happens inside me is almost more intense than the moment I first beheld Ita. My heart misses a beat, maybe two. Could *she* be the woman of my dreams?

It's a village. I know she's about three years younger than her brother Tamaz, who is my age, which would make her nineteen. While they've been into the store and I've seen them around town, I don't really know them. Tamaz and Mariam, as far as I know, were home schooled. They seem well groomed, not weird or inbred, and not unfriendly.

Fit and fluid, she ascends onto the buggy like an angel. She's dressed in a navy-blue frock, an overcoat, and a headscarf—not high Parisian fashion, but tasteful. Classy. Straight brown hair hangs to the middle of her back, parted in the middle, frames big brown eyes, and full, pouty lips.

My breathing shallows, my heart palpitates, and as our eyes connect, I permanently sear the vision of her into my memory.

I smile and wave as her papa whips the horses. Her gaze lingers on me for a few endless seconds, but then I'm not sure if she's still looking at me or if she's interested. In the next instant, though, she averts her eyes and rolls off toward their farm.

Like a catchy melody, I can't get Mariam off my mind. I consider venturing out to their farm, hoping that by some fortune she happens to be out in the vineyard where we can chat, but that seems creepy.

Instead, I slowly convince myself that she was an aberration and descend back into my pathetic, lonely life, stroking my violin, hoping that somehow, sometime, I will find happiness.

Herschel can tell that something is on my mind. One Wednesday afternoon, as I'm sweeping the store when nobody else is around, he says, "What's up with you?"

"Nothing," I say.

"Don't hand me that. Elazar, I know you. Your despondence has morphed."

I close my eyes and clench my fists.

"Who is she? Out with it!"

With trembling lips, I utter, "Mariam."

"Gabashvili?"

I nod, staring at my shoes. After a long pause, I tell him about the incident after her papa was in the store when we made eye contact.

"That's it?"

"I can't stop thinking about her."

"She's Georgian."

"Yeah." I swallow hard. "You can't imagine the power of that glance."

"I went down this path once…"

"Really? With whom?"

"Georgian women, from a young age, are told to guard their modesty, especially in traditional families like the Gabashvilis. It would take very little to ruin her reputation, so even if she is interested in you, she will play hard to get. She might be head over heels for you, and still reject you multiple times, or not show it all. This cat and mouse game seems to be the rule in Georgia—no girl wants to be perceived as easy."

"What should I do?"

"Don't be pushy or needy towards her. That won't be appreciated or get you results. You might be surprised at how far politeness, while persisting, will take you instead."

29 October, 1922 — Nearly a month goes by to no avail. The days are shorter, the weather is colder, and soon, winter will set in, which means we have practically no customers, the family hunkers down and endures the cold dark months, scarcely leaving the house, surviving off preserves and dried meat. And music.

Today, however, is Sunday; the day of the last farmer's market of the Fall season. All the vendors from around Kalarash will offer the remnants of their harvest. It's an annual event and if the weather cooperates, can have a festive atmosphere.

Papa, mama, Herschel, Sarah, baby Shimon and I bundle up and make an outing of it. While it's chilly, it turns out to be a clear, cloudless day and nearly the whole shtetl is in attendance.

The market is set up in Kalarash's town square. Booths surround the square selling everything from clothes to plants, baked goods to arts and crafts, and withering produce. A sizable crowd by local standards—growing by the minute—mills about the square.

Practically no sooner than we got here, Shimon starts crying. Hershel and Sarah take him aside to change his diapers. Papa and mama strike up a chat with some other friends from the Synagogue, so I venture off by myself.

I sally about the market for a good half an hour, poking through various booths, when out of nowhere, standing next to a flower stand, I see her: Mariam Gabashvili.

I gather myself, recalling Herschel's advice to be polite, yet persistent. With the calmest, most confident tone I can summon, I say: "Hi, Mariam."

"Hello," she says.

"I'm Elazar. Do you remember me? From the hardware store?"

She glances around nervously as if to see if anyone is watching or listening. She takes a deep breath, nods, and says, "Yes."

"Nice day," I say, "for this time of year."

She forces a smile and I detect she's about to walk away.

"It was nice seeing you the other day," I say. "Do you remember? I waved at you?"

"Yes."

"You're... looking very well."

"Thanks."

I take in her magnificence. I can't help but compare her to Ita—there are similarities in their looks. Maybe I have a type, visually, yet her countenance is much more down to earth, not as brash or elitist. Then I blurt, "What is your life's ambition?"

"Excuse me?" she says.

"I just don't want to trample your dreams. So, what do you want to do? Be a scientist? A musician? Move to Paris and become a famous artist?"

She laughs. "Other than distillation of alcohol, I know little of science. I'm not an artist. I'm a Georgian woman, born and bred. I want to find a man who I love and who loves me. I want to have a simple life together, keep a happy house, fix delicious food, and raise a loving family."

My heart melts. I say, "Me, too."

"Really? You don't have any… bigger dreams?" she asks.

"Yes. I mean… I, I play the violin. I've dreamt of moving to Odesa or Vienna and playing in a symphony. But, you know, papa says I'd end up working nights, playing birthdays, weddings, and bar mitzvahs. He's probably right."

At this, I can tell she deflates, and in my callowness, I'm unsure which part disappoints her.

"But I would be very happy to live a simple life and raise a loving family," I say.

"If only it were that… simple." She glances away and, in the distance, she sees her parents.

Sensing I'm about to lose her, I panic and say, "We should get together sometime. I don't know, maybe go for a walk. Get to know each other better."

"I… I really can't."

"Oh, come on. We could just be friends."

"That's very nice of you, but I have to go," she says, and walks off toward her parents.

CHAPTER 10

7 November, 1922 — More than a week later, I'm still trying to make sense of our encounter. Politeness? I don't know what else I could have done. Persistence? That's what all women want. What am I supposed to do? Go to her house and knock on the door? That's back to being creepy.

I leave it in God's hands.

That afternoon, I happen to be on the road in front of the shop when I hear a horse and buggy coming up behind me. I think little of it and simply move off to the side of the road to give it plenty of room, so I don't get run over.

As it passes, I look up and it's the Gabashvili carriage. Sitting on the back, looking my way, is Mariam.

I light up inside and give her a huge smile and wave.

To my surprise, she smiles and waves back.

I spread my arms and drop my jaw as if to say, "What do I have to do to get together with you?"

She glances back to make sure her papa isn't looking, and then beckons me with her finger to follow.

I mouth, "Now?"

She nods and beckons me again.

It's early afternoon and there's nowhere I must be for a few hours, so I slip away—I'm pretty sure unnoticed—as I watch the Gabashvili buggy roll into the distance in the direction of their farm.

I've never visited the farm, but it's no secret where it is. After about a thirty-minute walk up and down the rolling steppes of central Bessarabia, I take the dirt road I know to be their driveway and continue onto their estate. A grove of trees soon gives way to a vineyard that surrounds a large house – the former headquarters of the premier winery in our region. Perched upon an elevated stone porch, the imposing structure is fronted by nine Ionic columns connected by arches sprawling away from a three-story atrium above the entrance.

It's not the Kaplan mansion in Bolgrad, but with the land sprawling in every direction, this is bigger and, in some ways, more impressive.

From behind a bushy grapevine, I survey the property. There's no sign of their horse and buggy. There's no sign of anybody. Was I imagining things? Was she really beckoning me?

Marching up and knocking on the door seems like a bad idea, but if she's watching for me to show up, hiding is also not smart. I force myself to stand where I can be seen from the house and pray to God that I'm not about to die.

Just as I'm about to turn around and walk back home, a female voice whispers, "Elazar. Elazar."

I turn to my left and there, emerging from behind a row of grapes only a few meters away, is Mariam.

"Hi," I whisper back. It's more of a stage whisper, and I look around to see if anyone might possibly hear us, just as she closes the gap between us and gives me a hug.

"I'm so glad you came," she says.

"So am I."

"I didn't think you would."

"I almost didn't," I say, "but then I thought, how many chances in life do we get?"

"I was thinking the same thing."

"Uh… Are your parents here?"

"No. They took my brother to visit relatives. I told them I didn't feel well, and they let me stay." She looks me up and down and smiles. "In fact, there's no need to whisper," she says and stops whispering. "They'll be gone until late tonight. We're alone!"

I swallow hard and my heart does a flip. "How nice."

"Would you like a tour?"

"Absolutely. I would love a tour," I say.

"Come, come," she says, then takes my hand and leads me through an iron gate and up maybe thirty stairs to a spacious stone porch. Wooden wine barrels frame both sides of the stairway as we reach the top. We turn and take in a view of the countryside with Kalarash in the distance.

"Wow! What a stunning view," I say.

"Grandpa put a lot of thought into where to put the house, and pretty much every detail to put this property to its highest use."

I rest my hands on the waist-high stone wall, and a chunk of masonry breaks off as I pan the surrounding property.

"Oops," I say.

"Don't worry." She takes the rock and puts it back where it was. "The place is getting a bit old and requires constant upkeep, but the bones are good."

To the left is an orchard with various types of fruit trees. In front—the sunny side facing west—a large section of what looks like a previous vineyard has been converted to a vegetable farm. I follow Mariam to the right, southward, where vineyards continue as far as the eye can see.

"Welcome to the Kalarash Winery, which is known for its beauty and the abundance of fruit and vegetables it's capable of producing. It's one of the oldest wineries in Bessarabia, founded in 1896 by my father, David Gabashvili."

"He came here from Georgia?"

"Yes, from the capital Tbilisi. Georgia is generally considered the 'cradle of wine', as archaeologists have traced the world's first known wine creation back to the people of the South Caucasus in 6,000 BC. The early Georgians discovered that grape juice could be turned into wine by burying it underground for the winter. Some of the *qvevris* they were buried in could remain underground for up to fifty years."

"Why did your papa come here?" I ask.

"Because the unique climate and soil conditions here are favorable for the ripening of grapes and for the production of cognac. Using modern equipment, classic recipes, traditions, and inspired work—before prohibition—we were able to produce world-class products."

"Ugh," I say. "Prohibition."

"There seems to be a lot of that going on in the world."

"Your family is adapting. Finding other products to farm, ways to get along."

"Yes, but there are other prohibitions beyond alcohol."

"Like what."

"You know what I'm talking about," she says.

I know where she's going with this, but right now, to me, it's irrelevant. I say, "I can't stop thinking about you. I can tell that you are attracted to me."

"Be that is it may, it nonetheless remains true that… There's a cultural divide. You know it and I know it."

My vision blurs and my entire being boils. "I've spent my whole life in this shtetl, harboring the fear, resentment and hatred ingrained in me by my parents… spawned in them by what led up to the pogrom in 1903, what happened during and since."

We stare into each other's eyes. She doesn't say anything.

"But in my two decades, this hate has all been second-hand. I've never really known any Christians, and if *you*, this vision, this angel standing before me is what a Christian is, then I don't hate them. Quite the opposite is how I feel for you."

Mariam silently expresses her steadfast agreement, then, with a loud creak, opens a gigantic oak door revealing a stone staircase leading down into a deep, dark cave. She dislodges two torches from holders attached to the stone wall, hands me one, then her face illuminates as she strikes a match, lights her torch, and then my torch with hers.

Holding the torch, illuminating her eyes and her bushy dark hair, she looks—in a gorgeous, glorious, glamorous version of my interpretation—like a good medieval *baba yaga* witch. The musty smell of stagnant air and distilled spirits combine with the flickering light to raise my level of excitement.

"Want to see the wine cellar?" she asks.

"Yes!" I say, grinning from ear to ear.

"I've accompanied various guides on this tour countless times since I was a little girl. Now keep up," she says, leading me down into the depths.

"I promise," I say.

With the intonations of a seasoned tour guide, Mariam descends the stairs, saying, "Kalarash Winery has its own plantings of vineyards, the area of which is six hundred hectares. About one hundred thousand decalitres of wine distillates aged from one to twenty years are stored in these cellars. The products include more than twenty-five types of cognac, aged from three to twenty years, as well as brandy, other strong alcoholic drinks, and table and sparkling wines."

We reach the bottom of the stairs. I squint and we raise our torches as our eyes adjust. A wooden floor stretches maybe fifty meters into the distance beneath an arched-stone roof, separating on either side, two rows, one stacked atop of the other, of wooden barrels.

"This is amazing," I say, my voice echoing throughout the hall.

"Would you like a taste?" Miriam asks.

My mouth salivates. "Yes, please."

She goes to a tasting cask, produces two glasses, and expertly opens a valve, pouring two modest portions of the dark liquid into the glasses. Handing me one of the glasses, she says, "I hope you like cognac."

"I can't say that I'm a connoisseur, but I'm willing to try anything."

"Anything?"

"Almost."

We clink glasses, and I say, "Here's to us."

"To us," she says as we make eye contact and then both take a sip.

The cognac warms my innards and begins to calm my nerves.

"I've been thinking about you ever since that day I saw you climb onto your papa's carriage outside of our store," I say. And what guy wouldn't? My words have a choked, tortured quality.

"And I, you," Mariam says.

I lean across the wine cellar, my hands reaching for hers. She lets me take hers up, but she avoids my gaze. "I've never said this before, but my heart is hopelessly and irreversibly yours."

In the dimness of the torchlight, I see how Mariam's features pull tight across her dark, brooding face. She draws in a long breath, and she keeps me waiting several minutes before she responds.

Finally, her eyes find mine and she says, "When I think about all the reasons why you should not love me, about all the reasons why I should not love you, Elazar… all the reasons why it is foolish for me to love you." She pulls her hands away from mine as if, even here, they aren't safe.

I lean forward to reach for her, but she denies my embrace and I nearly explode with frustration.

"And there is an abundance of reasons I should not love you. I went to yeshiva, and I know it's a basic tenet of Judaism for a Jewish man to only marry a Jewish woman, but that is based on ancient—and, if you ask me, dubious—premises. For that reason, Mariam, in my heart, I see no point in torturing ourselves like this," I say, pressing myself to her. "You know I love you. I've tried not to. We both have, but some things are simply greater than either of us."

At last, she wavers, her resolve faltering as I grasp her, pulling her into my arms, and she willingly yields to my kiss. I run my fingers through her hair, pressing my weight into hers as we fall backward into the support of a nearby wine barrel. I hear my own breath, heavy, as it matches Mariam's. Our bodies, like our exhales, fold into each other, meeting in the dark in that most natural and necessary of unspoken languages.

CHAPTER 11

It's late when I get home. I've missed dinner, my timing is unlike any I've ever perpetrated, and my footing is a bit wobbly. Like beginning a nocturne, I inhale, quietly open the front door, and attempt to ease into the composition.

Halfway across the living room, I hear a scratch and then see the glow of a match bursting into flame. Sitting on the couch, papa takes three big puffs, lighting his pipe, and then blows a billow of smoke into the air and growls, "Where have you been?"

"Just, uh, out with some friends," I say.

"With whom?" he asks, blowing out the match.

"Just some of the guys from yeshiva."

He stands and lumbers over to me. "I've been watching your interactions with the Gabashvili girl. Both at the farmer's market and then this afternoon when you followed their carriage toward their farm." He sniffs me. "You smell of female and cognac."

"Papa, I'm twenty-two years old. I have needs. I don't have a lot of choices in this town."

"She's Christian," he says with disdain.

"She didn't participate in the pogrom," I say.

"Marrying outside the faith is *asur*, forbidden," he says.

"I won't let hate rule my life," I say.

"This is not about hate," he insists.

"Yes, it is," I say.

"Do you want to have a family?" papa asks.

"Maybe," I say.

Papa gives me a look of utter disgust.

"Of course, I do," I say.

"Do you want Judaism to disappear, to melt into the fabric of society?" he asks.

"No" I say.

"Then you're not marrying Mariam Gabashvili," he says. "If the mother isn't Jewish, the children aren't Jewish."

"In Genesis 21:13, God refers to Hagar's son as 'the son of the maidservant' rather than 'your, Avraham's, son'. Later, rabbinic sources deduce from this that a Jewish man's child is considered "his" child only if the mother is Jewish," I say.

"End of discussion," papa says.

"Yet in yeshiva, I was taught to think for myself, to question my beliefs… Abraham fathered children with three wives or concubines: Sarah, Hagar, and Keturah. According to Jewish tradition, Sarah was a member of Abraham's extended family, and her descendants became Jewish. Hagar and Keturah's descendants were considered non-Jewish. Is it okay if I have one Jewish wife who was my cousin and two concubines?" I ask.

"No," papa says. "Don't be silly."

"I could go on quoting all sorts of weird bases from Deuteronomy to Leviticus to Talmud from which Judaism established the law of matrilineal descent, and I find them antiquated, in many cases racist, downright weird, and—to say the least—dubious," I say.

"The law is the law. My grandchildren are going to be Jewish," papa says.

"Maybe," I say.

"Listen to me, young man," papa says. "If you marry a goy, I will disown you."

SECOND MOVEMENT
CHAPTER 12

13 April, 1923 — I am in the tool aisle five-and-a-half miserable, frigid months later, reorganizing a new shipment of hammers and trying to figure out what to do. When I ponder what would make me happy, I'm astonished by how contradictory my situation is. I have a good job I can keep for the rest of my life, but it feels like a life sentence.

One day I'll be the boss—the conductor. So what? I live in a place that feels like home, but it is home. My parents' home. All that would be great if I could find a meaningful relationship, but it seems I'll never find one if I'm living and working here.

"What's going on?" Herschel calls over when there is a lull, which has been all winter, but he has a way of finding lulls in whatever occupies his mind when I'm down.

I drop my head. Here we go again. "It's not complicated."

"Are the hammers not lining up?"

"In a manner of speaking," I say, adjusting our last sledgehammer one centimeter rather than, as I'm tempted, using it to smash the entire display.

"Oh. For a change can you just tell me what's bothering you?"

You are so dense, I think, but I try to cut him some slack. He's simple. He's married, has a son and a wife who is pregnant again, and he hasn't spent this endless, bitter cold winter sleeping months upon months alone in his broom in our parents' home and he pretty much only thinks of himself.

"Nothing that concerns you," I say.

"You're my miserable brother. I work with you. That concerns me," Herschel says.

"How about your half-ass work? That bothers me. Look at that shelf. That's not a display, it's a pile of tools. Now, as usual, I have the pleasure of arranging your mess, so this place doesn't look like a junk heap," I say.

"This isn't a haberdasher, you fuss!"

I try to squeeze past him in the aisle, but he blocks my way with his fat body in the same bullying way he has since we were little kids. I employ my usual spin move, avert his pedestrian antics, and start organizing the shelf.

"You know what your problem is? You're too picky," Herschel says.

"Fuck you," I say.

"Fuck yourself. Oh wait, that's what you do," he says.

"Do you really love Sarah? Or did you just marry her because she was handy?" I ask.

"I love Sarah," he says.

"Yeah? Well, I loved Mariam, but papa forbade me to marry her. Now she's already married her old boyfriend, moved back to Georgia, and that's not an option, is it?" I ask.

"Uh, no," Herschel says.

"Now, no one in this shtetl does it for me. Last summer, I met the *Jewish* woman of my dreams, and it turned out that I wasn't the man of hers. I guess you'll never have to feel that, so you'll never understand," I say. "But if you thought I was picky before, Ita—and Mariam— ruined me! I felt what it was like to be in love. Until I feel that happens again, it won't be enough."

"Maybe it was *bashert*, meant to be by God, that you shouldn't be with her because you are destined to be with someone else," Herschel says.

"Then God is cruel, and he is torturing me every day—every *night*—that I spend alone," I say.

We hear the front door of the store open and slam shut. I resume arranging the tool display while Herschel grabs a broom and starts sweeping.

"Elazar! Herschel!" Papa yells as he walks in. Herschel and I exchange glances; we both know something extraordinary is amiss.

"I have an opportunity," papa says.

"What is it?" I ask.

"David Gabashvili just returned from the Odesa. More political change is in the air," papa says.

"Like what?" Herschel asks.

"It's complicated… I'm not entirely sure, but that's part of what we're going to find out," papa says. "Let's say there are buying opportunities."

"Where?" I ask.

"Bolgrad," papa says. "Pack a bag, Elazar; you and I are going to Bolgrad."

CHAPTER 13

16 April, 1923 — Just like that, three days later, we're aboard a train headed for Bolgrad.

Part of me feels like a seasoned railroad traveler. It's Monday, a light rain is falling, and the coal smoke, swaying and constant hum don't nauseate me as bad as before, or at least, they're not unfamiliar. But traveling with papa is much different than going by myself. This is business. I don't foresee telling my grandchildren about how this was the trip that changed my life.

"There's so much I want to know, papa. I hope you will narrate the trip, point out landmarks and lecture me on the history of every bend along the tracks," I say.

Nice try.

It's a bit chilly as we depart—we're both wearing jackets—but in contrast to the heat and mature crops of summer, we pass endless, fertile countryside and farmland, swaths of brown budding into green fields germinating with wheat, rye, and corn.

After burning through two bowls of pipe tobacco, papa snoozes most of the way to Kishinev, and then, as we roll through, he lights his pipe again, but is silent and doesn't even look out the window.

I'm trapped next to him. I scrutinize papa's suitcases in front of us in the luggage bin, which I earlier found oddly heavy. I ponder an extra bag's inclusion along with my bag, another of his and yet another rucksack he's safeguarding under his feet.

I try not to think about Ita. I press myself to think beyond her. There's no way more than one goddess of my dreams was born in Bolgrad.

I pretend my right forearm is the neck of my violin and practice my repertoire of songs in silence, which is a habit that Herschel can't stand… as if his tapping everything in his flailing reach isn't more annoying.

I don't know how long I've been doing this when I notice that papa's eyes are open and he's watching me.

"You're a very gifted musician," he says.

I stop, flabbergasted. He's *never* said that with this conviction.

"Thanks."

"One of the things that hurts me the most about having left Kishinev is that you can't attend music school as I did," papa says.

For the first time, maybe ever, I think I see compassion in papa's eyes. He seems younger, more agile.

"At least you found Schmeul to give me music lessons," I say.

"It's not the same as a formal education!" he says.

I cringe as usual at his rebuke. Wrong again. So much for compassion. I lean my head against the window.

"Alas, I never made it to conservatory," papa says. "I could have been a conductor, a composer, a professor."

I sit up and look him in the eye. Maybe I was wrong that I was wrong. "What's important is the person, their talent; what God has given them. I mostly love how music makes me feel," I say.

Papa's eyes light up. "Music is the language of feelings because we have so many feelings that we don't have enough words to explain. Music has many more tools to explain what we feel. To be a deep human being, it is essential to study, as it deepens your ability to know what true love is."

I've heard fragments of this allocution, but I find it soothing and I feel a growing bond with papa like never before.

"If music wasn't a huge part of my life, I would be much poorer," he says. "Forget about money. When I play,

I share my feelings with the world. This is what it is about. I feel much richer, and I feel sorry for rich people who never have this experience."

He hugs me with one arm, and I rest my head on his shoulder.

"So, why are we going to Bolgrad? Why now?" I ask.

"You'll see."

We ride in silence for hours on end, and, like before, I'm glad I'm not on a horse or walking, but it's still a long ride. I finger my arm violin, playing scales, chord progressions and songs. Papa immerses himself in a book.

We look out the window as we pass a farm teeming with a vast flock of sheep. A shepherd and several dogs mind the flock and I notice a flicker of amusement in papa's eyes.

"What?" I ask.

Papa chuckles. "Never mind."

"Tell me."

"Don't tell your mama," he says.

"I won't," I promise.

"When I was your age, I knew a guy who grew up on a ranch. They had sheep, cows, chickens." He glances around to make sure nobody is listening, leans close to my ear, and whispers, "He claimed that he fucked everything on the farm except the hay loft, and he jerked off on it."

I burst into laughter, and almost choke to death, causing fellow passengers to glance our way. Never have I heard papa use such language.

He winks at me, elbows me in the ribs and goes back to his book.

I look back out the window at the passing sheep. Never again will I look at farm animals in the same way.

We drink water and eat food mama and Sarah prepared. We pee. My vision blurs as I stare at the endless expanses of farmland.

We arrive in the dead of night. Instinctively, I head for the park across the street, but papa leads me just a few blocks from the train station to a hotel.

The hotel is quaint. A fixture in Bolgrad, it's called The Hotel Inzov, and it is built from logs with a tile roof. It sits on a corner that connects Ukraine, Bessarabia, Romania, and Bulgaria.

Once we rouse the innkeeper, which takes some ringing of a bell on the desk, he finally appears in his pajamas, is nonetheless cordial, negotiates the terms of our stay, and directs us to our room, which is small but comfortable with two single beds. We undress and fall immediately to sleep.

CHAPTER 14

17 April, 1923 — The next morning, we have breakfast of kasha and tea in the dining room of the Inzov seated with other guests on carved wooden chairs at long wooden tables.

Fueled and rested, papa and I venture into Bolgrad, which is huge compared to Kalarash, but smaller than Kishinev. We walk the streets of the downtown—I know my way around since my first trip to Bolgrad— window shopping everything from clothing to shoes to household furnishings.

On the eastern edge of town near the railroad track we find a lumberyard. The sheer size of it amazes me, as does the variety and volume of its merchandise. We walk every aisle and exterior yard and chat casually with a salesman—a burly Jewish guy named Boris. He's very friendly and fills us in on the prices he has to offer.

Papa remains aloof. We start to leave, and I pull papa aside and say, "Aren't we going to buy anything?"

"What's the rush? We're here for a couple of days. Let's shop around, see what they have to offer. See what kind of deals we can get."

We continue our trek through Bolgrad, and I'm having a ball. It's so nice to be any place but Kalarash and actually having fun with papa. We eventually do our due diligence at a hardware store, which takes us the rest of the morning.

We have lunch at a diner downtown, and afterward check out a business that sells only tack.

By this time, my mind is in overload and so is papa's. We begin walking back to the Inzov, and I'm in a daze as I process all we have done. I stare at the sidewalk when, with a vocal inflection I've never heard, papa whispers, "Holy Moses, what have we here?"

Having no idea what he's talking about, I look up and see two women—clearly a mother and her daughter—coming toward us, but my mind is still occupied with the prices of bridles and bits.

I lock eyes with the younger woman.

As they get closer and their features become clearer, I say, "Oh, my God, papa. I can't believe my eyes."

"You know these women?" papa asks.

Nodding, I call out, "Hello!"

"Elazar?" the younger says.

"It's Ita and her mother," I utter out of the corner of my mouth. I spread my arms. Ita runs to me and gives me a hug.

I'm wetting myself, but I try to keep my wits. "Forgive me. Papa, this is Ita, the woman I've told you so much about. And this… this is her mother, Charna Kaplan. Ita, Charna, this is my papa, Toiva Gershovich."

We launch into a series of greetings and handshakes, and while we don't come out and say it, papa and I diffuse any notion that we might be in town stalking the Kaplan women, but rather, were in town on a buying trip and they say they just happen to be out shopping.

At last, Charna says, "If you gentlemen aren't busy tonight, we'd love to have you over to our home for dinner."

Papa looks at me. He's clearly intrigued, and I light up.

"We'd be delighted," papa says.

"Fantastic," Charna says. "I believe Elazar knows where our house is. We'll see you at six o'clock."

We stand in shock, watching as Ita and Charna walk away. I look at papa in his grungy black pants and shirt. I look at myself.

"We can't go to their house tonight dressed like this," I say.

"These are the only clothes we brought," he says.

"Who knew we'd be going to the Kaplan's for dinner?" I say.

At that, instead of heading straight back to the hotel, papa and I go shopping. "Good thing we didn't already spend all our money on hardware and building materials," papa says.

We wander the streets of downtown Bolgrad until we find a men's clothing store. We're greeted by a very kind Jewish man who is more than happy to guide us through a shopping spree. I've never seen papa in such a state. In a giddy sort of panic, we try on practically everything in the store and buy new outfits for the evening – including sport coats, shirts, ties, dress slacks, even socks, shoes, and underwear.

We go back to our room at the Inzov, hang up our purchases, enjoy a relaxing time at the sauna, shower, bask in the steam room, and flog each other with *veniks*.

Afterward, we go to our room and dress in our newly purchased clothes just in time to head to the Kaplan home.

CHAPTER 15

17 April, 1923, Evening — Papa opens the mysteriously heavy suitcase and gives me a wry smile as he reveals that's it's full of wine and cognac. In his rucksack, papa packs two bottles of the finest wine we brought from Kalarash. We check each other's new outfits.

"I don't think either of us has ever looked better," I say.

"I agree," papa says.

We hug each other, because we both know that *tonight* is one of those nights that we will remember for the rest of our lives.

On the walk from the hotel—about ten blocks—papa has a bounce in his step, and I feel a comradery with him like never before. Instead of dictator and underling, conductor and violinist, we're like colleagues, even pals.

When we arrive at the Kaplans', papa takes in the palatial structure with its Ionic columns and nearly has a heart attack.

"This is where they live?" he asks.

"I told you," I say.

"I thought you were exaggerating. It's a good thing we went shopping."

"Take a deep breath," I say, and I lead him up the steps.

Promptly at 18:00, we ring the doorbell, and after a long enough pause that I start to panic, Anica answers the door. She leads us into the cavernous living room, where Charna and Ita greet us.

Ita wears a loose-fitting dress with an almost straight bodice. The dress features an asymmetrical skirt hem, which is slightly ruffled, where one side is longer than the other and the shorter side is decorated with a bow on the hips. The dress is sleeveless and has a V neckline. Charna's dress is similar only peach-colored, decorated with sequins, and also sleeveless, but has a plunging U neckline.

"You both look stunning," I say.

"Thank you," Ita says. "It's the latest fashion from Paris."

Papa presents Charna with the wine we brought from Kalarash, for which she is delighted, and we are swept into the living room and sat on the couch before a coffee table set with platters of cheese and charcuterie.

Anica takes the bottles, pours a dry wine made in Bolgrad in crystal glasses, and we settle in, chatting about our day exploring the hardware and tack stores of Bolgrad, our shopping spree, and our time at the sauna.

Ita and Charna counter with challenges of maintaining the home, Ita's triumphs during her first year at art school, her latest paintings, and how thanks to correspondence with Ita's sisters in Paris, they're up to speed on the latest in French fashion.

Just after 19:00, Anica announces dinner is ready, and we repair to the dining room, where the end of the lengthy dining table that was closest to the kitchen was set with the finest crystal, silver, and bone china. A flower arrangement and candles separate us from the reaches of the table, making the setting for four warm and intimate. Anica pours more white wine, and while Charna fills us in on the history and culture of Bolgrad, Anica brings out a salad of tomatoes, cucumber, onion, and fresh feta dressed with vinegar and olive oil.

Papa raises his glass and says, "I'd like to propose a toast. Here is to you, Charna and Ita, thank you very much for your kindness and hospitality."

We all clink glasses and sip our wine.

I take a bite of my salad and my taste buds go wild. "This is the best feta I've ever had. It's fresh, and not too salty," I say.

"It's made here from sheep's milk," Ita says. "Sheep breeding is an important occupation in Bolgrad and the surrounding villages."

"I've heard that," I say, and my mind fixates on the word "breeding," replaying her inflection, its implication and how it was formed by her mouth. I resist vocalizing the story papa told me on the train, but then I'm sure Ita is reading my mind and I blush as we both suppress snickers.

Without interrupting the conversation or ever making us wait, Anica seamlessly keeps the dinner moving and never lets our wine glasses get below half-full.

Charna continues, "Huge plantations in the Bolgrad region were farmed before prohibition as vineyards. Since the time of the Greeks, Bolgrad wine has been known for its winemaking far beyond Ukraine."

"As is true of Kalarash," Papa says. "In fact, our close friends, David, and Katherine Gabashvili, own the Kalarash Winery. Or they did, until it was closed in 1915, but they still own the land."

I cringe when papa refers to them as our close friends, but I keep my mouth shut.

"Oh my God! You know the Gabashvilis?" Charna asks.

"Yes," papa says. "They live just up the road. They're clients at the hardware store, and our children are about the same age."

"Wow! It is such a small world. We're old friends, too," Charna says. "We've sold them fabric for curtains, home furnishings… All sorts of things. They stay with us when they come to Bolgrad."

A vision of Mariam in her wine cellar floods my mind. I push it away.

Anica switches us to red wine poured into larger glasses to pair with the main course of lamb chops, roasted potatoes, and green beans. We sip wine and talk about how, under prohibition, the vineyards are sitting fallow, and how the Gabashvilis have switched to farming fruit and vegetables and doing surprisingly well.

As we savor the last bites of our main course, our conversation turns to Ukraine.

Charna heaves a great sigh. This rouses papa.

"Are you well?" he asks.

She's silent for a minute, and I think that perhaps she has declined to answer. Then she sighs again. "Toiva, you oblige me with your concern. I am well enough, but all is not well in Ukraine."

"Oh?" papa says.

"In truth, things could not possibly be worse," Charna says.

"We've heard bits and pieces," papa says.

I look at him in disbelief, as this is news to me.

I say, "Living in Kalarash, we're pretty isolated."

"I will try to explain," she replies. "I've tried to articulate this before, but the words don't seem to form as they should."

I sit waiting, glancing into Ita's eyes. I can tell she's tempted to chime in, but we all wait, determined not to press Charna.

"The nuances will undoubtedly escape you, and I don't have the heart to explain them in detail," Charna says. "Nor do I even have all the facts, filtered as they are through garbled radio reports, blotted letters, and second-hand accounts."

We nod for her to continue.

"The Ukraine of my youth is no more," Charna says. "A famine set in motion by years of war, and now drought and crop failure, has beset the country." The information comes from her mother, who lives in Mariupol, and who, with her father, are also vintners in the wine regions of Southern Ukraine. "My family… My parents, siblings, nieces, and nephews are starving. Many of my nephews have been shot."

I stare at her in horror. Papa reaches out his hand, but withdraws it as she keeps her palms pressed against her temples as though trying to contain an explosion.

She provides us then with an outline of Ukraine's woes. Since 1917, Ukraine has been fighting pro-Bolsheviks desperately trying to avoid Soviet rule. It's gone back and forth, the Poles have been involved, and it's been mass bloodshed. Now, aided by a drought, grain yields are down more than seventy-five percent compared to 1916, and the Soviets are using it in their relentless desire to take over Ukraine, which is the main source of food for all this part of the world. Via violent military expeditions, the Soviets requisition grain reserves that could have avert the famine. Along with starvation, millions are dying of fever, typhus, typhoid, and cholera.

Again, I am nonplussed. How could this be happening not that far away and we, in our shtetl cocoon, are oblivious?

Charna continues, "And now Russia—the communists—led by some Georgian schmuk, Losif Vissarionovich Dzhugashvili, who changed his name to Joseph Stalin, is finally taking over, and to me it is as if Ukraine is being eaten by its child."

We talk about Ukraine becoming a part of the Soviet Union, how throughout history, Ukraine has been invaded from the west and the east all the way back to Greek times, and more recently has been ruled by Cossacks, Russians, Austral-Hungarians, and Ottoman-Turks. It goes on and on.

Now, Charna tells us about how her family's business—her livelihood—is also being taken over.

"How can they do that?" I ask.

"It's a vast undertaking, but it's happening," she says. "The biggest fish, closest to Moscow, are going first. We had an office in Moscow. That went first. Now, they're taking over landowners, the biggest companies—you could say the biggest threats—and they're working their way down. Or that's what it looks like is happening. And it's coming this way."

"But Bolgrad is part of Romania," I say.

"Yes, but geographically, it's right in the crossroads of where Ukraine and Romania come together, and many businesses here are afraid that it's only a matter of time until Stalin will take over Bolgrad."

"And?"

Charna pauses for a long time while avoiding eye contact with anybody. "The worst thing now is they have sealed the borders. Travel to western Europe is no longer possible."

At this, my entire being does a flip as I see tears well up in Ita's eyes.

"This can't be true," I say.

"Surely this travel ban will go away soon," papa says.

"One can only hope," Ita says, but I can see doubt in her eyes.

We change the subject back to happier days as we savor dessert of fresh fruit and cream.

After dinner, we repair to the living room and have a digestif of Bessarabian cognac. I cradle the glass in the palm of my hand and sit close to Ita while papa moves closer to Charna, and what had been one conversation becomes two.

The night is a pleasant one this close to the Black Sea, and Ita opens the doors that lead out to a terrace, where sounds of the early-spring evening seep in from the darkened gardens.

"Might I suggest we take these outside?" I say, raising my glass. "The request of a peasant, you'll have to forgive me. I'm more comfortable out of doors than inside these posh quarters."

I offer Ita my arm and she accepts it with a checked smile as we step outside. I wonder if she can feel the slight trembling in my frame emanating from both my arousal and the alcohol. I realize it's both, compounded by the fact that while the music of spring is swelling in the garden, it's a bit chilly, and we're not wearing jackets.

She clearly knows what I'm thinking and says, "Why don't I show you my latest painting, and we can let the grown-ups remain in the living room solving the world's problems?"

We go to her studio and… from there, I'm pretty sure we kiss. There is passion between us, though I've had more to drink than I ever have, and from there the night fades into haze.

CHAPTER 16

18 April, 1923 — I come to the next morning, fully dressed on the couch in Ita's studio. My bladder's ready to explode, and my head pounds as I struggle to recall what transpired before I lost consciousness.

As if she somehow senses that I'm awake, Ita enters, her quaffed evening dress replaced with a yellow sundress and sandals, and says in a cheery voice, "Good morning."

"Good morning," I say.

She smiles, gives me a peck on the lips, and sets a cup of tea on the cluttered coffee table in front of me.

"Last night was amazing," I say. "Thank you so much for your… gracious hospitality and scintillating conversation. The food was amazing, and… what happened?"

"You slept well," she says.

"But… what happened?

"Don't you remember?" Ita says with a mischievous smile.

"No. Not exactly," I say.

"Fear not. We didn't do anything we'll regret," she says.

I have many regrets—especially all the things we could or might have done that we would regret—but I keep them to myself. "What about papa? Your mama?"

"They're fine," Ita says.

"Fine?"

"They're in the breakfast room. Join us when you've had a chance to freshen up," she says and disappears out the door.

Over more tea and pastries, I study papa who concedes that he and I have much work to do in the hours to come, and after many words of thanks, we schlep back to our hotel wearing our slightly rumpled new clothing in silence. I'm dying to ask what transpired with him last night, but he isn't volunteering any information, so I don't pry, because I suspect that he has similar curiosity, but I keep quiet as well.

At the hotel, we change into our work clothes, hang our new ones carefully in the closet of our room and set ourselves to the business at hand. It's called barter.

First stop is the lumber yard, where Boris is happy to see us return.

"Hello!" Boris says.

"Hello," papa replies.

"What can I do for you?" Boris asks.

"As you could see from our perusing yesterday, we are interested in the wares you have to sell," papa says.

"I gathered that. What do you have in exchange?" Boris counters.

"Well, I have cash and other negotiable items, but we could start with this," papa says, and shows him a portion of the wine we brought from Kalarash."

"You've got my attention," Boris says.

We walk through the store, tagging stacks of lumber, bricks, and other building materials. Papa gives the salesman an idea of how much he is willing to pay, and the two negotiate the largest transaction they can, during which time I watch closely and am surprised by how cheap the prices are, but keep my mouth shut.

As papa pays, my eyes bulge as I see for the first time the contents of the bag he's been so jealously guarding since we left home: everything from old 20-lei gold coins, French francs, and Turkish gold lire to wads of more-recent paper lei in various denominations he pulls out of his rucksack, and arranges to have the order shipped to Kalarash.

From there we go to the hardware store, where papa plays a similar tune, starting with plying the salesman with alcohol and then proceeding to negotiating the rest of the transaction and as before, shipping to Kalarash included.

CHAPTER 17

18 April, 1923 — On the train home the next day, my head boils with what I learned on the trip.

"How are you?" papa asks.

"All this talk about Russia taking over, is that why you and I are here?" I ask.

"Yes. As you could see, the businesses here—which are an integral link in the supply chain from Bucharest to Kiev for hardware and building-materials—want to liquidate what they have now so that they can convert them into gold, precious gems, or other commodities that they can hoard, so they can secure what they've worked their whole lives for before the Soviets come in and take it all away."

"That's why we got such good deals on hardware and building supplies?"

"You've got it, my dear boy. We are going to make money like never before."

"But…"

"But what?"

"Where did that bag of money come from?" I ask.

Papa takes a deep breath and stares out the window at the corn fields blurring by. "This is not a new process."

"Explain," I say.

"The only true path to freedom in this world is self-sufficiency," papa says.

"Okay," I say.

He looks away again, then puts his hand on my thigh, looks me in the eye and says: "You're going to have to pay somebody taxes, that's for sure, so the goal there is to minimize what you pay, whatever it takes. After that, you want to own your property; paying rent just makes other people rich. You never want to be in debt, or you are your debtor's slave. If you can own your property AND have enough money to support yourself and your family, then you can do whatever you want."

"Easier said than done," I say.

Papa glances around to make sure nobody is listening.

"Since I was your age, I have saved every leu I could, and then I have it converted into gold, precious gems, or good old-fashioned cash, and I hide it someplace where nobody can find it. And that way you have a back-up plan. You're not going into debt or slaving away for some tyrant."

"I get it. Now the merchants in Bolgrad—and their suppliers— are doing the same thing to ward off this impending Russian threat," I say.

"And now it's time for us to up our game."

My mind reels. "But can we sell what we're buying?"

"Yes, that's where what Charna was saying last night about Ukraine is another piece in the puzzle. We still have a Romanian border protecting us, so while there is hardship in Ukraine, there is increased demand for the farmers around Kalarash like the Gabashvilis, the Egorovs and the Axelrods. We're not talking huge numbers, but in our little world, they're expanding and wanting to buy as much building materials as they—as *we*—can get our hands on."

I'm silent for some time as my body sways with the train and now I stare at the fields whizzing by. "So, here is our chance, in our scale of business, to make as much money as we can. Liquidate, convert and hoard."

"Yep," papa says.

"But that also means that there is a good possibility that… eventually the Soviets will take us over, too."

"That's the scary part."

We both go silent for a long time. In my mind I replay the evening with Ita and Charna, especially the part about Russia taking over Ukraine and closing the borders to travel.

I put my head on papa's shoulder and say, "Ita still has three-plus years of art school left, but it's starting to seem unlikely that she will ever get to go to Paris."

"I didn't want to say it at the time, but I'm pretty sure that's what we were all thinking," papa says.

"Is it possible that my love life may be the beneficiary of the swing of Russian politics?" I ask.

"That's the way it looks."

"I am truly disappointed for Ita, but inside I'm overjoyed. Is that bad?"

"No. It's life."

My whole body convulses, and I suppress tears as we ride in silence for a long time, maybe half an hour. From time to time, papa and I glance at one another. I can tell that there is joy and a concoction of other emotions boiling inside him.

"What happened with you?" I ask.

"When?"

My head sags forward. "At the Kaplan's... during the stretch of time, let's see, between when I passed out... and when I met you for tea in their breakfast nook the next morning."

"Oh, that stretch of time," he says.

"Yes."

"Let's see." He scratches his head. "I... I slept."

"Where?" I ask.

"In a bed in their house," he says.

"In a bed? In what room?" I ask.

"A bedroom," he says.

"And you slept?"

"Yes."

"Is that all you did? Did you sleep alone?" I ask.

Papa drops his head and stares at the floor. "Do you really want to know?"

"Oh, my God. I can't believe this," I say.

"Take it easy," papa says.

"You cheated on mama?" I ask.

Papa takes a deep breath and then flaps his lips as he exhales.

"You had sex with Charna?" I ask in a raised voice, and several people look our way.

"Keep your voice down," papa says. "Calm down."

"Calm down?" I ask. "You're the one who has always lectured me on monogamy and being true to your wife. How could you do this?"

"We didn't plan this; we just ran into them. She was lonely, I was lonely, there was alcohol involved… and sometimes life isn't as simple as you think," he says.

"Wow. I can't believe I'm hearing this."

Papa's silence is like a full pause, where the melody of his sonata moves from iron to silk.

"You dog," I say.

"You just wait until you've been married for thirty-four years, have been through a pogrom, and been banished to a shtetl. I've worked very hard to build a life for you and Herschel and your mama. And we have a very good life! But that doesn't mean…"

"What?" I ask.

"That I have a sex life," papa says.

"You and mama don't have sex?"

He shakes his head.

"Why?" I ask.

"Women aren't into sex… they just want children, and then they're done. You'll understand more when you get older. But the best thing we can do now—for me, for you, for Herschel and his family, for all of us—is keep this between you and me, because I love your mother, and this doesn't change anything."

"Have you had other… indiscretions?" I ask.

"No."

"Okay. Okay," I say, though I'm having trouble buying it. "This is going to take some time to process. But I guess… we'll just have to put our heads down, do our hoarding, and as the threat of Russia looms large, we'll see if we can maintain self-sufficiency."

Papa puts his arm around me, gives me a half-hug, then presses his forehead to mine. "Yes."

"And… we might be forced to go to Bolgrad on more buying trips?" I ask.

"Wouldn't that be awful?"

CHAPTER 18

July, 1923 – For the next three months, Ita and I write to each other at least once a week, keeping up on the mundane details of our day-to-day lives.

Papa and I share the story about running into the Kaplan women with mama—we had to explain our new clothes—and having dinner at their home, but we never breathe a word about the rest of what happened. I think she suspects something, but she doesn't ask.

Mid-month, I ride the train from Kalarash to Bolgrad on a buying trip.

Papa does not accompany me.

When in Bolgrad, I get up early and fix myself breakfast and always clean up after myself.

During the day, I am out on buying calls, attending to business.

Never underfoot.

CHAPTER 19

22 August, 1923 — At last, a little over a year since we met, Ita and Charna come to Kalarash.

I rent a horse and carriage and pick them up at the train station. We make our familiar greetings, gather their luggage, and I chauffeur them to our property. I drive them up Strada Alexandru cel Bun and past warehouses, toward the center of Kalarash. A hill rises to the east above the green Kalarash valley, while the strada runs parallel to the railroad track as well as a creek, which runs through the southern border of town.

It's a warm afternoon, and the trees that line the street create a gentle, Jewish entrance to the shtetl that enchants—or possibly horrifies—the Kaplan women. It's not Bolgrad.

Less than a kilometer later, we arrive at our place: a two-story house next to a gray store on a corner with a sign above the door that says *Gershovich's Hardware and Tack*.

I pull back on the reigns and say, "Here we are."

"So, this is the place I've heard so much about!" Charna says.

Mama and papa stand on the porch watching as we roll up and pile off the carriage. Herschel and I unload the luggage.

Ita and Charna are both happy to see papa, but we all know that this trip is about affording Ita and Charna an opportunity to bond with mama. Much to my surprise and relief, I detect nothing awkward on anyone's part when I make the introduction.

"I'm so happy to finally meet you," mama says.

I ensconce the Kaplan women into our guest bedroom—formerly Herschel's bedroom—then escort them on their initial tour of our empire, as it is, including our house, the hardware store, lumberyard, and warehouse that backs up against the railroad track. Neither is unimpressed.

Papa and I fix a roaring fire in the living room and play a few accordion-violin duets while Ita and Charna help mama fix supper. When it's ready, we all sit down to a salad of cucumbers, onion, and tomato with feta cheese as a first course, followed by cabbage stuffed with ground beef. The dinner is delicious, and our thirsts are quenched with water and tea.

The women do most of the talking, exchanging ideas about cooking, fashion, homemaking and the like, and I am just happy to be in Ita's presence. When he's finished eating, papa fires up his pipe and, like me, enjoys the presence of the women.

After dinner, papa, mama, and I—despite lacking Herschel as our percussionist—entertain the Kaplan women with several songs.

Ita and Charna are clearly tired after their long journey, so we all retire early.

As we bid each other good night, mama makes an announcement, "We've all been invited to the Gabashvili's for dinner tomorrow night."

CHAPTER 20

I stand alone in the garden, the familiar space barely recognizable as I survey the scene. David and Katherine Gabashvili have conjured their very own Eden at the Kalarash Vineyard, with heaps of sunflowers, dahlias, pinks, and lilies. Papa ordered a massive arrangement delivered for the dinner, accompanying the garlands of hibiscus and honeysuckle that drape along the banquet table in the garden.

David pours generously from his wine cellar and feeds us lavishly. As the night deepens around us, the air is redolent with the aromas of not only the flowers, but also the feast—lamb, beef saffron rice and stewed apricots.

The night is balmy with just the slightest breeze, and though the mockingbirds sing and the whip-poor-wills chant, we hear none of those summer sounds, for Katherine has hired musicians for the night.

David invites several of our family's most important clients—the Egorovs and the Axelrods—and looks on as the man of the vineyard, approvingly. Katherine flits about in her gown of blue silk, tossing orders at the servants and accepting the compliments of the guests. She's been nervous about a summer rain, but the night settles around us clear and comfortable, and the relief is evident in her broad smile.

After dinner, the band begins a new set and I approach Ita, tap her on the shoulder and say, "May I?"

She barely places her hand in mine before I'm guiding her forward into a swift quadrille. Like our first dances at Leo's wedding, our steps are decisive and self-assured.

Nearby, papa laughs, the sound of his joy soars over the din of the partygoers and the music.

"He is happy," Ita says, keeping her eyes fixed solely on me.

"So is your mama," I say. And she is, and for that I'm happy too.

But my head swirls with thoughts. First of what happened that night in Bolgrad between my papa and her mama, and then my heart carries a pang of sadness, thinking of my night in the wine cellar on this estate, knowing that my feelings were vanquished by a decree from my father, or right now it might not be Ita I'm dancing with. I try to push all this messiness aside and tell myself that is *bashert*.

"Mama likes you," Ita says, her pronouncement pulling my thoughts back to the present. I steal a glance across the garden, where Charna sits, smiling, flanked on one side by mama and papa and on the other by the Axelrods and the Egorovs, Bessarabian allies contemplating our region's fate.

"She does?" I ask.

"She thinks you're a dear boy. From a respectable family."

I nod. I suppose that's good.

Without premeditation, the following words spew from my heart, "When you and I are married I want to have a party even grander than this."

Ita nearly tumbles into the soft grass, but fortunately I'm holding her up, guiding her through the dance steps.

When you and I are married.

There has been no proposal.

"Did I say that?" My heart pounds and my face flushes crimson red.

"Yes, you did," Ita says, suppressing a smile.

"I… I didn't mean for it to come out that way. I… I was thinking it, but I would never be so presumptuous as to say such a thing without first making a proposal in a well-thought-out place and a carefully planned time."

At this very moment, a waiter passes us carrying a

tray of full wine glasses. I grab two and hand one to Ita. We stop dancing and I pull her away from the commotion.

I say, "Kindness and a winning smile cannot be beaten, but ambition and a positive attitude are also important. I want someone who likes physical activity—a good dancer—who has a good intellect—maybe even a brilliant artist—who can carry on a conversation, and who enjoys the process of getting to know someone first rather, than jumping in just to be with someone. A sense of humor is also important, especially when dealing with differences and misunderstandings. Nothing is nicer than someone who can laugh at themselves without sarcasm taking over."

A soft laugh rumbles inside Ita as she looks deep into my eyes.

I continue, "I prefer a relationship that is an equal partnership. The trick is to find someone whose imperfections don't drive you mad, and who can tolerate yours, and someone who knows how to push your 'happy' buttons.

"Ita, you do all those things for me, and in the end, it is the chemistry that decides the strength of the connection, and I believe ours feels good. You cannot make someone love you, it either happens or it doesn't."

I raise my wine glass and say, "Ita, you are everything to me. I can't live without you. Will you marry me?"

Ita takes a big swig out of her glass, swallows, and with tears running down her face, says, "Yes!"

I drain my glass.

We kiss.

CHAPTER 21

1923 to 1926 — I can't imagine how I will survive for three more years without Ita; without a girlfriend in Kalarash. The winters are endless, while the summers are busy, warm and all too short.

Business is good, as papa predicted. With famine and hardship in neighboring Ukraine, demand, and prices for produce—especially on the black market—are high. Farmers and most businesses in and around Kalarash thrive, making business for us good as well as our clients—the Gabashvilis, Axelrods, Egorovs and the like—who can maintain and upgrade their properties.

This makes it necessary for me to make multiple buying trips to Bolgrad. I stay with the Kaplans, but in the guest room, and I long for the time when Ita and I are married.

Papa and I do all we can to prepare for when that time comes.

One day, papa comes to me and says, "Our family's savings are at an all-time high."

"Yes, I know," I say. "Don't you think there might be a better way of securing it than burying it in the back yard?"

"A two-story apartment building just came on the market. With the money we've saved as a down payment, and with our cash flow, I think we can afford to buy it, and even pay it off in a relatively short time. That will give us all income for our retirements," papa says.

I wholeheartedly agree. And so in addition to managing the store, I have a new project of managing our apartment building. I keep it as a surprise to Ita, but on the top floor of the 8-unit building there is an apartment that I steadily fix up for Ita and I to live in when we get married.

CHAPTER 22

May 28, 1926 — Somehow, I survive three more years of loneliness, and in the final spring, I make the long trip to Bolgrad, this time so that I'm there when Ita graduates from the Bolgrad College of Art with perfect marks. Charna, Riva, and Rachman are also in the audience to witness the event.

Charna fixes us a nice dinner after the commencement, and I raise my glass. "To Ita. Congratulations on your amazing accomplishment."

Everyone raises their glasses and toasts, but my heart sinks when I see sadness in Ita's face, which, in turn, diminishes my happiness in being there and a part of her life.

In a moment of bitterness that has been brewing for some time, I say, "Pity it's not what it might be, were your dreams intact and were I not still in the picture."

"Stop it," Riva says. "That's not fair."

"No," Ita says, "It is fair. This isn't what I hoped tonight would be, but the world isn't fair."

"No. It's not," I say, tempted to get up and leave.

"But that doesn't mean I don't love you. If the borders weren't closed and I still could go to Paris, would I go without you? I don't know. We'll never know. But it is the way it is, and we are here now, and I am very grateful to have you."

"And you will happily move to Kalarash?" I ask.

"Yes, I will."

"And what about you, Charna? Aren't you disappointed that you aren't moving to Paris to be with your daughters?"

"No," Charna says, "that was never the plan. My life, my friends, my empire are all here in Bolgrad."

Rachman adds, "My family, my life, my job… they're all here in Bolgrad."

"I don't want to go to Paris," Riva says.

"The plan has always been for me to stay here," Charna says, "with Riva and Rachman, to help them raise Bene."

"I love you, Elazar. I want to be your wife," Ita says.

CHAPTER 23

9 July, 1926 — Ita steps off the train six weeks later on a sunny Friday, at long last arriving to marry me, to live the rest of our lives together in Kalarash. As I wave, my heart melts as Ita waves back, takes her mama's hand, and they both quiver with excitement.

I run to Ita, take her into my arms, and say, "Hello, hello. I've been dreaming of this moment for so long."

"Thank you. I'm very happy to be here."

"Thank God! Welcome. Welcome to your new home."

Behind her, Charna, Riva, Rachman, and Bene disembark, and behind them, a bittersweet void in the absence of her sisters, Fania, Tanya and Alya. But if they were here, Ita might not be. I shake the thought from my head.

Herschel, Rachman, and I load a mass of steamer trunks, suitcases, and boxes onto a carriage.

"Wow! How much did you bring?" I tease.

"All of my worldly possessions." Ita blows me a kiss, then grabs Bene's hand as he slips away from his Riva.

Mama, papa, Herschel, Sarah, five-year-old Shimon, and three-year-old Yakov stand on the front porch when we arrive, framing an epic moment.

Everyone exchanges greetings and talks at once, until I raise my hands along with my voice and say, "Riva, you, Rachman, and Bene will sleep in the store. It's not bad; the store was originally a small house. We set up a bed in what was a bedroom in the back. The three of you will have some privacy. The back door is open. Make yourselves at home. Dinner will be ready at six o'clock."

"Perfect," Riva says.

Rachman, who holds Bene on his hip, nods in agreement. He hands Bene to Riva, grabs their bags, and they go to the store.

"Okay, Charna, you and Ita, like last time, will stay in our guest room in the main house. Please follow me."

I kiss Ita. She and Charna secure their purses and a small bag, then Herschel and I grab two larger bags each and we all schlep into the house.

For the rest of the day and all the next, the Gershovich property buzzes with a blur of preparation. The men and I clean out a spacious warehouse behind the back property near the railroad track, where we set three long tables in the shape of a horseshoe that opens to the center of the room. The women spend the afternoon cooking a mouthwatering dinner for Shabbat, which we all enjoy together and bond as a family.

10 July, 1926 - On Saturday, we put up a *chuppah*—a canopy beneath which Jewish marriage ceremonies are performed—in the center of the warehouse, while the women spread white tablecloths on the table and set it with our silver and china, and put new candles in the candelabras. Remembering the night at the Gabashvilis' when I proposed to Ita, mama and I attempt to create our Eden with heaps of sunflowers, dahlias, pinks, and lilies, and likewise we drape garlands of hibiscus and honeysuckle along the banquet tables.

Leaving much of the fluffing to the last minute, the women then set about preparing the food for our wedding feast.

Anna and Leo stop by Saturday afternoon, as well as Aunt Rosa, as do friends and people from all sides of the family as they arrive from all over.

11 July, 1926 — On Sunday morning, the Kalarash *banya*—on both the men's and women's sides—is crowded with members of our wedding party. Among others, Leo joins papa, Herschel, and I while we shower, enjoy the steam room, and flog each other with *veniks*.

Likewise, Ita, mama, Sarah, and Anna visit the *banya* early, then spend the rest of the morning at our house beautifying. Their laughter and chatter echoes through the house as they do their nails, fix their hair, and apply make-up of smokey eyes and dark lips.

We time everything perfectly so that by wedding time—15:00—guests are filling the warehouse-transformed-into-a-wedding-hall as a photographer captures the arrival of all the guests, the band, and all the meticulous decorations.

Anna, who wears her hair in a short bob and sashays about in a pink flapper dress, says: "The flowers are amazing... the tablecloths... everyone's clothes... I love the palate of your wedding!"

In the main house, papa, and I—along with Leo as our official witness—meet with the Rabbi and sign the *Ketubah*, the legal formalities, with all of us wearing black suits, white shirts, gray ties, and *yamakas*—skullcaps.

When we complete the formalities, we walk across the backyard and wait at the entrance to the warehouse/

synagogue, as the Rabbi walks down the aisle to the chuppah, signaling the official start of the ceremony. The guests, including the Gabashvilis, Egorovs and Axelrods, about thirty in attendance, fall silent.

All reservations, fears and doubts evaporate from my soul and, escorted by my parents, I seemingly float on air through the wedding hall, catching the eyes of all the people I cherish the most, to the chuppah.

I squeeze both of my parents' hands, gratefully look them each in the eyes, and then we all turn.

My heart nearly beats out of my chest when I see Ita. Those eyes that captivated my heart at Leo's wedding still are, and will forever be, the portals of my love. My eyes drift south to the string of pearls adorning her neck, then plunge with her neckline and reside on her decolletage. Her magnificent radiance is softened by a sheer veil that falls over her shoulders as it flows down her back nearly to the floor. How can I be so lucky as to have caught this magnificent songbird?

I spectate as Ita grasps her Mama's hand, proceeds through the gathering of adoring onlookers, and joins me. Our eyes lock. We bask in each other's aura, inhale, and turn our attention to the Rabbi.

"Shalom! Welcome! Please be seated," the Rabbi says. "It is with a joyous and light heart that I welcome you to this moment, the wedding of Elazar Gershovich and Ita Kaplan.

"What are we all, but a series of moments strung together to create a lifetime? And just like a flip book where the pictures come together to create movement, our life's moments move just as quickly. Blink, and you'll miss them. Turn your attention away from the present, and you'll miss the whole thing.

"Marriage signifies an important change. Not just in the lives of the couple, but also in the lives of their friends, families, co-workers, and everyone whose life this couple touches.

"When was that first moment you noticed your one true love? When was that first moment you realized that this was the person you did not want to live without? When was that moment you look at your true love and thought, 'This is my forever?'

"For Elazar and Ita, this moment, here, right now, is one I hope they will remember fondly for the rest of their lives."

Ita and I relish every word and blessing of the ceremony, and I know that she means it deep in her heart when she says, "I will."

I look deep into Ita's eyes and say, "With this ring, you are made holy to me, for I love you as my soul. You are now my wife." I slide the ring onto her finger.

The Rabbi says, "Life is made up of moments. Live within those moments. Cherish those moments. Time is often thought to be our most precious gift, but I believe it is time spent with our loved ones that is the most precious gift of all."

He continues, "And so, enjoy each and every moment you are together, and keep one another in your hearts in those moments you are apart."

The Rabbi turns to the congregation and says, "And now we come to the breaking of the glass. I've filled the glass with all the negative paths and possibilities your marriage could have had. Once you break it, you'll only be left with positive and blessed moments. Even when times seem tough, remember that you'll get through them and get back to joy, because this glass is about to be broken."

The Rabbi places the glass under my foot. I raise my hands as I crush it, and everyone yells, "*Mazel tov!*" meaning congratulations/good luck.

"I am proud to announce that by the power vested in me by God, you are now wed. You may now kiss as I and everyone here wishes you Mazel Tov!"

I kiss Ita with every fiber of my being, and with this connection I know my heart is betrothed for life.

Rachman and Herschel take away the chuppah, and a band begins to play a fast folksong.

The whole new Gershovich/Kaplan mishpaha dances and drinks together. We feast on a spread of Kalarash's finest wine, sturgeon, salmon and roasted beef with sage and apples. After our guests have eaten their fill, I stand beside my new bride at the driveway to the lumberyard and see them off, waving happily at the line of departing carriages.

"Are you happy?" I say, pulling Ita close to me.

Ita cries tears of joy. "This is the best night of my life."

We retire to The Hotel Kalarash, an old, three-story building in the center of the shtetl, just a short carriage ride from our property. When at last we're checked in, standing in our room, Ita turns to me, takes my hand in hers and says, "Alone with my husband. At last."

I smile. *At last.* She's correct. I'm twenty-six years old! How long have I lamented the fact that marriage seemed like a doorway through which I had been barred entry? I squeeze her hand in return.

"My wife."

I carry her to our bedchamber and make a grand gesture of bearing her over the threshold. She feels nubile and supple in my arms as I lower her onto the bed.

"Well then, Ita."

She looks up at me, her blue eyes alight. "Yes, Elazar?"

"You make me feel a bit shy," I say.

She tugs on my shirt, pulling it over my head as I lift her dress. My mind swims in a heady whirl of wine and giddy feelings—nervousness, eagerness, even a bit of bashful modesty—but I gasp when I see her bare skin for the first time.

"Do you find me attractive?" she asks.

I study her body, taking in the soft curves of her flesh, her supple arms, expansive chest, strong shoulders. Her skin fairly hums with desire, and so, I realize, does mine.

"I find you sublime," I answer honestly, leaning forward to meet her lips with mine.

Ita offers me her body and proves any fears I might have had wrong with our first, long kiss as man and wife. There's certainly no lack of passion between us. I take her in my arms with a strong, determined embrace, and lower myself ever closer until there is no more fabric or modesty to separate us. There is no more conversation this evening, at least not of the spoken kind.

We spend the next day and night at The Hotel Kalarash, barely emerging from our bedchamber and our newlywed joy. Meals are brought on trays and enjoyed in bed. We care very little for exploring the grounds or the large rooms of the hotel, so consumed am I with acquainting myself with my new wife's body and the previously unknown pleasures she seems so intent to pull forth from mine.

After our brief stay as man and wife at the hotel, we relocate to our new apartment not far from our store in Kalarash. I don't look at the new place as we approach, but rather watch Ita as she sees it, as my reaction can only be formed once I see that she is happy.

"Here we are, my beloved Ita," I say as our carriage pulls up to our new building. A stairway leads up to a second-floor entrance tucked away from the street. As we enter, the apartment is brightened by tall windows with a balcony overlooking an inside courtyard. The apartment has three bedrooms, much larger than we need for the two of us, but it will be perfectly suited for entertaining and, I think, a growing family.

"Does it please you?" I ask.

"Oh, Elazar, it's wonderful. I thought we'd be living with your parents," she says.

"I couldn't see us living that way," I say.

"So… we're tenants?" she asks.

"Actually, no," I say, detecting a confused look on Ita's face. "We're resident landlords. Papa and I bought this building. We will live here, manage it, and it will provide income for our retirement."

I smile now that I see her happy expression.

Inside, the apartment has as-yet sparce furnishings, but is a work in progress. It's nowhere near as lavish as her home in Bolgrad, or even my parents' house, but I know that we can be very comfortable here as we oversee the decorations and furnishings together.

I whisk her up and carry her toward a room in the back of the apartment. "Where are we going?" she asks.

"Where do you think? I say, my eyes lit with a rakish twinkle. "To our bedroom, of course. That drive was far too long."

She giggles. "Oh, you need a rest?"

"I said nothing about resting," I answer, picking up my pace. I kick the door open. In the center of the room is a full-sized bed made with feather pillows and blue bedcovers. There's a mirror and a dresser, from which comes the soft click of an oak tabletop clock. I turn us toward the bed and say, "Time to christen our marital chamber."

I lie Ita down, the plush pillows absorbing our bodies as we laugh, and I struggle with my boots and clothes. "I might need your help in shedding all these trappings," I say.

"I am happy to serve you," Ita says.

We spend a delicious afternoon together, oblivious of all else that happens in the apartment house or the outside world. Afterward, we lay in each other's arms, and I use my finger to trace a gentle line up and down Ita's bare, goose-pimpled back.

"The tenants must think we are mad," I say, chuckling. "We arrive, and yet they barely catch a glimpse of us."

"We *are* mad," Ita says, rolling toward me. "At least I am. I am mad for you, Elazar."

"And I love you. I know this isn't the life that you dreamed of, but please allow me to make you happy, because I do love you, more than I ever imagined possible."

During Ita's first week in Kalarash, we hang one of her paintings over the buffet in our dining room and others throughout the apartment.

Ita sets up an easel in a corner of the kitchen, where there is also a built-in desk that she and I will use as an office.

When Ita isn't painting or doing other chores and I'm not working in the tack shop, I show her all over the town I call home.

In mid-December there is snow on the ground and frost on the branches of the trees. On Friday nights, Ita, mama, and Sarah fix Shabbat dinner at my parents' house, as is now routine, for the whole Gershovich family.

While Ita peels carrots for dinner, she catches Sarah and mama whispering to each other and looking at her stomach. She pretends not to notice.

As people arrive, Ita and Sarah light two candles.

Once dinner is on the table, Ita takes her seat across from me. I look her deep in the eyes, as if non-verbally confirming her permission. She grins and nods. Everyone is talking, so I tap my wedding ring on my glass.

"Excuse me, everyone."

"Quiet, please," mama says.

When the chatter stops, I raise my glass and say, "Shabbat shalom. It's wonderful for our family to be together. Tonight is special, because Ita and I have an announcement to make." I pause as the room goes silent. "There is going to be a new member of the Gershovich Family! Ita is pregnant!"

"Mazel tov!" papa says, raising his glass.

CHAPTER 24

1926 to 1940 – These are the happiest, least traumatic fourteen years of my life.

On June 25th, 1927, Ita gives birth to a beautiful girl, whom we name Rivka, after my beloved grandmother.

This sets in motion the era of parenthood for Ita and I, and we relish every milestone: when Rivka learns to crawl, utters her first word, learns to walk…

Three years later, on March 15th, 1930, we are blessed with a second child, this time a boy—more milestones— whom we name Ira after Ita's father.

A girl and a boy! *Oy vez mir*. In the eyes of God, we clearly are doing something right.

We live in relative prosperity raising our two children, and I slowly take over the management of the store and the apartment building. With rents and profits from the store, we pay off the apartment building and begin to enjoy steady income like never before.

Our love grows like a symphony, with crescendos and decrescendos bringing beauty to every minute we share together.

She paints, and I play my violin solo and with the family band. Yes, papa still reigns as the conductor, and I'm perfectly okay with that because with it comes responsibilities that I'm content to let him shoulder.

And through the years, together with the whole family, we spend Shabbat, Rosh Hashanah, Yom Kippur, Sukkot, Shemini Atzeret, Simchat Torah, Hanukkah, and Tu B'Shevat.

Oy.

CHAPTER 25

Sept. 1940 — Boom. Fourteen years later, and I enter the kitchen holding a rolled-up newspaper just as a fly buzzes past my face and lands on the breakfast table. I swat at the fly but miss.

"I rarely used to miss killing flies," I say, "but it seems all of a sudden that I'm missing a lot."

"Maybe it isn't just you," Ita says as she pours me a cup of tea.

I'm now forty years old, Ita's thirty-six, and, well, we're both getting older. Our clothes are tighter, we show some gray hair, and we both need glasses to read. Ita places the kettle on the stove and yells down the hallway, "Rivka! Ira! Get up. You'll be late for school."

But it isn't just us who are changing or our children that are aging. The rumblings from Russia, the relentless push in every direction by the schmuck from Georgia, have been getting closer day by day. All attempts at turning a blind eye or denial are officially futile. Today the whole world is… unfolding. I unroll the newspaper like I do every morning, place my glasses on my nose, and take a sip of tea.

My eyes grow wide, and even though it's been coming for a long time, now, in black and white, it's official. I nearly spit out my tea. "Did you see this?"

Overnight, the format—everything about the newspaper—has changed.

"See what?" Ita says.

"It's different. I feel like suddenly I'm living in a different city. A different country."

"What's different?"

"The paper. Format, design… everything. Now it's called *The Truth.*"

"Isn't news supposed to be the truth?"

"Listen to this: 'The Soviet Union has liberated Bessarabia from Romania.'"

I stop and try to recall my history. "According to my papa, we were part of Russia since… 1812, when the Turks ceded us to Russia. Then we formed a union with Romania in 1918 during the chaos of the Russian Revolution."

"The way I heard it," Ita says, "is in a secret agreement that year signed along the Treaty of Buftea, the German Empire allowed Romania to annex Bessarabia in exchange for passage of German troops toward Ukraine."

"Russia saw it as an illegal occupation. And now it's officially over," I say.

"Now we're denizens of the Soviet Union," Ita says.

"Everything now belongs to everybody. Everybody is equal," I say.

"Really?" Ita shakes her head.

Rivka rushes into the kitchen. Already thirteen years old, she's becoming a woman in every way, and while she's tiny—barely 150 centimeters tall—she fills the room with joy. Pushing back dark, wavy hair that falls around her beautiful face to her shoulders, she spots the fly buzzing around my head.

"Good morning, Rivka," Ita says.

She held up her finger, takes the newspaper from me, rolls it up, and expertly smashes the fly just as it lands on the table.

"Good shot!" I say.

She smiles as she sweeps it into a dustpan, dumps it into the trash can, and hands the paper back to Ita. "Good morning," she says as she grabs a bread roll and takes a huge bite.

I look over my glasses and grin as she swallows the roll in two big chunks and chases it down with a glass of grape juice.

"Take it easy, Rivka; you'll choke," I say.

"I'm late!" she says.

"You're young. You have all the time in the world" I say.

"I don't know," Rivka says. "Maybe I'm trying to do too much. What with painting, choir, and debate and all my other subjects. And boys. And… everything! My life is so hectic. It's hard to keep up."

"Just try to enjoy it," Ita says.

"You're very lucky," I say.

"Lucky? Ugh. I don't get to spend enough time painting! Then sometimes I'm not sure if I'm any good. Am I wasting my time?" Rivka asks.

"No. I love your latest painting," I say.

"Sometimes I think people just say that to be nice," Rivka says.

"It's beautiful," I say.

"You are very talented. Better than I was at your age," Ita says.

"Maybe someday I can live your dream, mama," Rivka says.

"Yeah," Ita says.

"Really. I want to move to Paris and become an artist," Rivka says.

"Wouldn't that be fabulous?" Ita asks.

"Don't ever stop dreaming," I say.

Rivka wipes her mouth, leans over, and kisses me on the cheek. "Thanks, papa." She hugs Ita. "I have to hurry, or I'll be late for choir practice."

Collecting the picture, she gingerly puts it into her portfolio and hurries out the door.

"Love you," I say.

"Be brilliant," Ita says.

I shift my attention back to the newspaper and shake my head as I read another article. "People are dancing in the street."

"They love Stalin," Ita says.

"Well, you have to hand it to him, he keeps prices stable. He keeps the railroads clean and running on time. They claim he will protect us from foreign invasion," I say.

"Under communism, everybody knows what to do," Ita says.

"It sounds good," I say.

"In theory."

"So, everybody's equal, right? How's that going to work for Rivka? If she wants to be an artist, well, not everybody is equally talented as a painter or in any art form. Will she still be allowed to pursue it?" I ask.

"It's hard to say."

"The same is true in any line of work," I say.

"It sounds to me like the communists want to take from the rich and give to people who don't want to work."

"What's going to happen to our business? This apartment building? What about my parents' house?"

"I don't know," Ita says.

"And what's scary is… I've heard rumors brought on the tail of a magpie… that Michael Egorov has disappeared," I say.

"Disappeared? What do you mean?" Ita asks.

"He's gone. Along with his whole family."

"Where?"

"I don't know."

Ita is clearly rattled. "Did they move?"

"All of their belongings are still there, just no Egorovs," I say.

"People don't just disappear."

"I know." I gulp down the rest of my tea. I look at an empty spot at the table. "Where's Ira?"

Ita yells down the hall, "Ira, get up! You'll be late for school."

"Rivka's running her tail off and we can't get Ira out of bed," I say.

"He's ten years old," Ita says.

"That's no excuse."

"Our kids have such a tough life."

CHAPTER 26

October, 1940 — A statue of Lenin appears in the town square. City Hall gains new bureaus, from the Governor General's office to Ministry of Internal Affairs, which control police and fire services, as well as the NKVD—the People's Commissariat for Internal Affairs. Soldiers arrive by train and establish a military installment. Everywhere, there are strange faces on the street.

Posters are plastered all over town that read:

Attention, comrades of Kalarash. On Saturday, Oct. 5, 1940, at 18:00, all citizens are summoned to the civic amphitheater to attend a public Soviet Orientation Rally.

The same announcement appears in the newspaper.

"What if we don't go?" I ask rhetorically.

"I don't think we want to find out," Ita says.

"More news from the tail of the magpie," I say.

Ita's eyes get big. "What?"

"I'm officially terrified," I say.

"What happened?" Ita asks.

I take a deep breath and say, "Now the whole Gabashvili family has vanished."

"No! Not the Gabashvilis. This is getting awfully close to home. What is going on?" Ita asks.

"Apparently, it happens in the middle of the night," I say. "A black van pulls up, a team of police or NKVD or, I don't know, men in black uniforms storm the house and just haul everybody away."

"Why? What did they do to deserve it?" Ita asks.

"It seems to be people who could be perceived as anti-Soviet in some way, like Romanian policemen, prison guards, clerks, former military officers or, in David and Katherine's case, large landowners," I say.

"Where are they taking them? What are they doing to them?" Ita asks.

"Nobody knows."

5 October, 1940 — Ita, Rivka, Ira, and I arrive early for the orientation rally, when hardly anyone is at the outdoor amphitheater, and claim our seats in the tenth row, left of the center aisle.

I am relieved when my parents arrive shortly thereafter with Hershel, Sarah, Shimon, and Yakov. We make a big hubbub as we greet each other, and I say, "All present and accounted for. Thank God."

As a family, we sit and watch the people filter in.

"It's freezing," Rivka says, rubbing her hands together to warm them.

"Button up your coat," Ita says, pulling Rivka's collar together.

"I feel an energy in the air not unlike before a sporting event," then I whisper into Ita's ear, "But the feeling is rooted in fear. Fear of…"

Ita puts her hand over my mouth. "Don't even say it."

By the appointed time, the amphitheater is packed.

An orchestra, complete with a choir, assembles on the stage between the flag of the Soviet Union to our right and a huge portrait of Joseph Stalin to our left. The crowd goes quiet, watching a man in a black tuxedo walk to the middle of the stage, step up to a podium, raise a baton, and prompt the orchestra to play Tchaikovsky's Moscow Cantata.

Next, the orchestra plays the latest version of the Russian National Anthem, toward the end of which the newly-appointed mayor of Kalarash—a fat, balding Russian with a bushy mustache—steps up to the podium and takes the conductor's place as the music ends.

"Welcome, comrades. Welcome to the Soviet Union!"

The crowd cheers.

Pointing to his left, he says, "This is the flag of the Soviet Union. Its red color is the international symbol of the communist movement. The hammer represents the industrial workers, while the sickle represents the farmers, the union of which represents the victorious and enduring revolutionary alliance."

The crowd cheers again, louder.

"The star above the hammer and sickle represents the rule of the communist party. What does that mean? Well, that's what we're all here to get to know."

I squeeze Ita's hand.

"Everything now belongs to the government, which means it belongs to everybody. Healthcare will be free and available to everyone. The same with education."

More cheers.

"Just keep doing what you've been doing. The only difference will be that instead of working for whomever it was that you worked for, you now work for the people. It's that simple. Mostly, we just called you here to ask you to cooperate."

"The textbooks at school are all in Russian!" Rivka says. "Classes are taught *only* in Russian."

"We're supposed to learn a new alphabet and to speak this awful language overnight?" Ira complains. "Not one word is anything like Yiddish. Or Romanian."

"It's the same for all the kids in Kalarash," Ita says.

"Sure, easy for you to say. *Kak dyela*? Come on, mama," Rivka says. "How do you respond?"

"I made a batch of cookies. Would a cookie make it better?" Ita asks.

"No," Rivka grumbles, taking a cookie and biting into it. "I hate Russian, Russians, Russia, and everything it stands for."

"Your mother and I have to learn it too," I say. "We'll all have to make many adjustments."

The room goes silent.

"Stalin keeps the prices stable," I say.

"The trains are clean and running on time," Ita says.

"Everybody knows what to do," I say.

"But what's next?" Rivka asks.

CHAPTER 27

6 December, 1940 — Snow falls outside. A fire burns in the pot-bellied stove, and I count cash receipts from the shop at the kitchen table.

"Looks like it was a good month," Ita says.

"What difference does it make?" I ask.

"It was just an observation," she says.

"I work just as hard, maybe harder now than I ever did before, except now I have to turn over all of it to the Soviet office," I say.

"We get to keep a percentage, right? They pay for education, health care and pretty much everything else," Ita says.

"And our rent. But overall, we're making a lot less and have a lot less discretionary money than we did before," I say.

"At least we're not at war. I read that General Molotov met with Hitler and Ribbentrop in Berlin to discuss a New World. Germany is bombing England," Ita says.

"Where does it end?" I ask.

"At least we get to stay in our home," Ita says.

"So far," I say.

"We still have our jewelry, our silver and our crystal," Ita says.

"And our apartment building?" I ask.

"Poof," Ita says. "Now it belongs to everyone."

"That was income for our retirement," I say. "Our whole lives we've worked so hard and saved our money so we could purchase the building and in our spare time we've maintained and managed it. Now? Gone."

"Ukrainians live in the Synagogue," Ita says. "The Christian church is a warehouse."

"Friday night is just Friday night," I say.

"They haven't taken our children or your parents!" Ita says.

"Yet," I say.

"What about my mother? My sisters? What's happening in Bolgrad? In Paris?" Ita asks.

"I don't know."

"I feel so… powerless."

"Stalin will protect us," I say.

"Please, God," Ita says, adding, "oh, wait, we don't even have God. They're taking him away, too."

"We have our family, and we have each other," I say. "That's all that really matters."

Third Movement
CHAPTER 28

22 June, 1941 - 16:00 — **"This is All-Union Radio transmitting 'News from Moscow'. Stay tuned for an important announcement."**

Papa, mama, Ita, Rivka, Ira, Herschel, Sarah, Shimon, Yakov, and I, our whole mishpaha, gathers around the radio in our living room in Kalarash.

Static crackles, then, *"Vinemanye. Vinemanye. Gahvareet Moskva..."*

"Attention, attention, Moscow is speaking. We are transmitting an important government message. Men and women of the Soviet Union, today at four o'clock in the morning, without any warning or declaration of war, the German army attacked the borders of the Soviet Union. The Great Domestic War of the Soviet people against the German fascist invaders has started.

Our cause is justified, the enemy will be defeated, and victory will be ours!"

"Holy Moses," papa says.

"I need to change my shorts," I say.

"What in God's name is Stalin doing right now?" Herschel asks.

"Scrambling," mama says.

"Facing a massive task," I say.

"Oh. My. God," Ita says.

"We're going to war," mama says.

"I don't want to lose my sons," Sarah says.

"I don't want to die," Shimon and Yakov say in unison.

"I have two sons and not one grandchild!" Sarah says.

"Stop it, Sarah!" Herschel says. "Now is not the time."

"This could be the end of our family," mama says.

"You must survive this war!" Sarah says, hugging her boys.

"What about you?" Shimon asks.

"I don't know. How will we contribute? Where will we go?" Sarah asks.

"Calm down," I say. "Maybe this is a false alarm."

"Please, God," mama says.

"Then again, what if it's not?" Ita asks.

"Wait for further instructions," I say.

17:00 — An hour later, again on the radio we hear, "*Vinemanye. Vinemanye. Gahvareet Moskva...*"

"**Attention, attention, Moscow is speaking. Stand by for a speech by Vyacheslav M. Molotov in his capacity as the People's Commissioner for Foreign Affairs on the occasion of the German invasion, Operation Barbarossa.**"

There is more static, and then:

"**Citizens of the Soviet Union,**

"**The Soviet government and its head, comrade Stalin, have ordered me to make the following announcement:**

"**Today, at 4 o'clock in the morning, German troops entered our country, without making any demands on the Soviet Union, and without a declaration of war. They have attacked our borders in many places, and have subjected our towns—Zhitomir, Kiev, Sevastopol, Kaunas and some others—to aerial bombardments, during which more than 200 people have been killed or wounded. Hostile aerial attacks and artillery barrages have also taken place on Romanian and Finnish territory.**

"**This attack is unheard of and is a treacherous act that has no equal in the history of civilized people. The attack on our country was launched despite the fact that a non-aggression treaty between the U.S.S.R.**

and Germany has been signed, and that the Soviet Union has observed all conditions of this treaty in full honesty…"

Russia has faced seemingly unsurmountable foes before.

"The government calls on you, citizens of the Soviet Union, to close the ranks around our triumphant Bolshevist party, around our Soviet government and around our great leader, comrade Stalin, even further.

"Our cause is just. The enemy shall be defeated. Victory shall be ours!"

CHAPTER 29

23 June, 08:00 — The next morning, our store becomes a mad house. The milk man, the blacksmith, and two firemen show up first and buy everything they can get their hands on: rope, tack, rucksacks, camping equipment, tools, and kerosene.

"We all need to calm down. It's going to be okay," I say.

"Okay? Did you hear Molotov's speech?" the milkman asks.

"Don't overreact," says the blacksmith. "The Germans would be attacking a 3,000-kilometer front. It's inconceivable that they would have enough soldiers to wage such an offensive."

"Then why are you buying all this stuff?" Herschel asks.

"Just in case," the blacksmith says.

"If Germans are on their way, the Romanian border is only fifty kilometers west of here," one of the firemen says.

More customers come in. Thank God I have my family to help. Mama and papa are old—in their 70s—and in the back of my head I'm really worried about them. What are they going to do?

In a lull in the madness, I pull Ita aside. "Go in the house and prepare to flee. In the warehouse I think you can find eight rucksacks. Pack one for each member of the family."

Later, after the store is closed, together we steal away to our broom closet, lift a rug, and pry up a floorboard. We extract a box from the space beneath it, from which we pull out several un-cut gemstones, an amber ring, eight gold nuggets, four pairs of semi-precious earrings, Ita's pearl necklace and some costume jewelry she can't bear to leave behind.

In the dining room, we open the hutch and pull out our sterling silver collection: three sterling silver platters, two candle sticks, a candle snuffer, two nut dishes, a tea pot, a sugar bowl, a cream pitcher, and a heavy silver spoon. I strain under the weight of our silverware box, which contains service for twelve people.

Ita sews concealed pockets into our rucksacks, into which we stow small valuables. The larger silver items we distribute among each rucksack to keep the weight of each sack to a minimum.

Working with mama and Sarah, we calmly and thoughtfully fill the remaining space in all the rucksacks with food, clothing, medical supplies, and everything we can think of that might come in handy but that would not be too heavy to carry.

Ita leaves to deliver two rucksacks to mama and papa and two to Herschel and Sarah.

I look at my violin. There's no room for that.

"You heard Molotov. The government is calling on all Soviet citizens to mobilize against Germany. There is no question that there will be a draft," I say.

The room goes silent as I scan the Gershovich *mishpaha* assembled for dinner. All are in attendance.

"Shimon is twenty years old. I'm eighteen. We'll be the first to go," Yakov says.

"And what about you and Herschel?" Ita says.

"I don't know. I… I'm forty-one, he's forty-three. What's the cut off age?" I ask.

"They can't take me," Herschel says, pointing at his leg.

"We don't know!" Ita says.

"What happened to the non-invasion pact?" papa says as he raises his fist.

"If the Germans are invading, the government has to have been aware of a buildup of troops along the western border," Herschel says.

"Now there is lots of non-information. Nobody knows what's really happening or how bad the Germans might hurt us," Ita says.

Everybody starts talking at the same time until I hold up my hands.

"Calm down. Everybody! They're still a long way away, and I really don't think the war is going to come to this small town of Kalarash," I say.

"Don't be so sure," Sarah says.

"In the vastness of Russia, this is a low-priority place to attack," papa says.

"Can I suggest something?" Ita says. The room grows quiet. "If the Germans come, they'll be coming from the west, so if we have to run, it will be to the east."

Mama gives papa a look of despair.

Ita continues, "In case that happens, and we get separated, we need to have a plan. We need a place to meet."

There's a deathly quiet pause as everyone absorbs the gravity of what Ita said out loud.

"We don't want to go toward Kishinev; it will certainly be a focus of bombing," Ita says.

"Most people will probably take the road toward Bravicea," Yakov says.

"I say we hump it due east to Voinova," Ita says. "About ten kilometers up that horse path, in the next valley, is the Kirilenko's farm. Does everyone know where that is?" Ita asks.

Everyone nods.

"It's agreed. If we get split up, everyone meets there. At the Kirilenko's barn," I say. "But most likely, that will never happen."

"I hope you're right," papa says.

"Now everybody come get some food and stop this unpleasant conversation," I say.

"Dinner is ready," Ita says.

Ita keeps the radio on all the time for the next several days, hoping for news that the conflict was overstated and has been resolved.

We tend to the frenzy of business in the shop, raising prices amidst dwindling supplies. I can't think of anything else but try not to bring it up. Finally, I say, "This big announcement and then nothing."

"It's been days, and still there have been no new announcements," Ita says.

"Stalin has yet to address the Russian people about the war," I say. "When is he going to weigh in?"

CHAPTER 30

27 June — I turn on the radio as soon I wake up. Within minutes, I'm filled with dread when I hear the same voice that announced the initial attack:

"Attention. Attention. Moscow is speaking. In response to the German invasion, Russia is mobilizing for war. All men between the ages of eighteen and sixty are hereby ordered to report to their nearest recruitment center. This is a mandatory draft. Everyone must report on Monday, 30 June."

Everyone in Russia is aware of the announcement within hours of the radio address. More radio addresses, local newspaper accounts and flyers posted hastily by assembled recruiters in every city detail where and when men are required to report for the draft.

30 June, 08:00 — Herschel, Shimon, Yakov and I arrive at the Soviet Army recruitment office, which is set up in the gymnasium at Kalarash High School. There is already a line out the door of men waiting to be processed. Being obviously younger, Shimon and Yakov are told to wait in a different line than us older men.

The waiting begins. In the coming hour, we watch the line behind us grow until it circles the block.

An hour later, we make it inside the recruitment center, and another hour later we finally reach the front.

We're given questionnaires, upon which we fill in our names, dates of birth and other personal information and, upon completion, turn them in to a clerk.

We are ordered to strip and stand in another line naked. After nearly another hour, we're examined for lice, venereal disease, and a litany of other maladies.

Once we're finished with the inspections and dress, an officer toots a whistle to get our attention and says, "Sometime in the next day or so, you may find out if you've been drafted or otherwise assigned by checking for your names on lists that will be posted on the bulletin board outside the recruitment center. You are now dismissed."

Herschel and I get home first, and the store is busier than ever. Ita and Sarah are relieved that we returned, and that they have help with the rush.

Sarah brakes into tears when Shimon and Yakov come home. Their heads have been shaved, and they still have clips of cut hair on their shoulders.

"How did it go?" Sarah asks.

Wide-eyed, Yakov says, "We were questioned, given physicals and…" He starts to cry.

"We're going to war," Shimon says.

"We have two days to put our things in order. Our train leaves Wednesday morning," Yakov says.

"To where?" Herschel asks.

"Kishinev at first," Shimon says.

"Then we don't know," Yakov says.

2 July, 07:00 — The shelves at *Gershovich's Hardware and Tack* are empty. I leave the "Closed" sign in the window and make sure the door is locked.

Mama, papa, Herschel, Sarah, Ita, and I accompany Shimon and Yakov to the train station. It's a humid, overcast day, and Shimon and Yakov—like so many other young men on the street—wear recently-issued olive-drab combat fatigues, knee-high leather boots, and green helmets.

We wait around making small talk for more than an hour, as the train is delayed.

When the signal comes, we all take turns hugging the boys. "How are you doing, baby?" Sarah asks Shimon.

"I'm sick to my stomach. I'm not going to lie, I don't want to go to war. I don't want to die. I promise I will do everything I can to survive, return, and give you grandchildren."

"Oh, Shimon." Tears stream down Sarah's face.

"Right now, we have no choice but to go to war," Yakov says. "I'm ready to do my part to stop Germany."

"Come on, boys," Herschel says. "It's time."

"Goodbye," Sarah says, brushing away tears as she kisses her sons goodbye one final time.

"Take care," Shimon says, maintaining his composure as he lets go of his mother's hand. He and Yakov join a mass of other recruits and board the train.

"I love you!" Sarah calls after the train, and she cries as it pulls away from the station.

On the way home, Herschel and I stop at the recruitment center. After fighting my way to the bulletin board and squinting through my glasses, I find my name on a list that is headed "white ticket."

I run back and find Ita and Sarah. "I got a white ticket!"

"What does that mean?" Ita asks.

"It means I'm excused from military service due to health issues. It came up in the interview. It is because I'm flat-footed, near-sighted and asthmatic."

Ita hugs me. "Never in my life have I felt so relieved to have an imperfect husband."

I smirk.

She musses my hair and kisses me.

"What about Herschel?" Sarah says.

I point to a crowd of men around a bulletin board. "He's still looking for his name. It's hard to read, and they're not in any particular order."

At last, Herschel limps out of the throng with a huge grin on his face.

"White ticket?" I ask.

"Yes!" he says.

"Me, too."

"I was exempted, obviously, because I am lame. Thank God! Something good came from the pogrom."

"We'll all still have to be involved in the war effort, but how remains to be seen," I say.

CHAPTER 31

09:30 - When we get back to the store, mama and papa go to the living room while Herschel and Sarah return to their apartment. Ita and I lock the door to the shop, leave the "Closed" sign up, and I go behind the cashier's counter and pull out the cash box.

I hug Ita with one arm and kiss her on the forehead as I open the metal box, pull out a thick wad of cash and raise my eyebrows. "Hmmm. It seems that Hitler effectively liquidated our inventory."

"How nice," Ita says, deadpan.

I count the money, make a mental note of the amount, and fan the cash. "This is more than we usually make in a year."

"Are you going to trot it down to the Soviet office?" Ita asks.

"Of course, I am," I say with a wry smile.

I go to the bedroom closet, remove a piece of floorboard, and extract the rest of the money and treasures that there wasn't room for in the rucksacks, and add it to the cash box.

I'm just about to leave the bedroom when in my mind an even more valuable treasure calls out to me like a comrade about to be left behind: my violin. I tear up, grab it, and, on a gut hunch, I make a trip downstairs into our basement.

Ita follows me to the far corner and asks, "What are you doing?"

"I won't be able to take it if we must flee," I say as I stick it in a closet in the far corner. "This way, if I ever return there will be a remote chance that it will still be here."

Ita shrugs. "Why not? You never know."

On the way back upstairs, I grab a spade and then take the cash box into the backyard and make sure no one is watching. Measuring two paces from the corner of the house, I stick the spade in the dirt and dig a hole about sixty centimeters deep.

Ita meanwhile counts the money again, takes a small fraction of it, holds it up and says, "This should cover our immediate needs."

I nod.

Ita secures the money, puts the rest back into the box and hands it to me.

I put the box in the hole and am about to shovel dirt on top of it.

"Hang on a minute," Ita says, and runs into the house.

She returns with a full, one-liter bottle of vodka and hands it to me. "This is to celebrate when we come back."

"Please, God," I say as I take the bottle. It just fits into the cash box with the rest of the contents. I close the lid and place the box into the hole. I carefully fill the hole with dirt and smooth the spot so nobody would ever guess anything might be buried there.

I brush the dirt from my hands, then hug and kiss Ita.

CHAPTER 32

3 July — **"Stand by for an address from the General Secretary of the Communist Party of the Soviet Union, Joseph Stalin."**

"It's about time. It's only been eleven days since the Germans attacked," I say.

"What took him so long?" Ita asks.

"Comrades! Citizens! Brothers and sisters! Soldiers of our army and navy!

To you I turn, my friends…"

"That's a first. I've never heard him refer to us as 'friends' before," I say.

"Shh."

"The treacherous military attack by Hitler-Germany on our motherland, which was launch on June 22nd, continues. Despite heroic resistance by the Red Army, and although the best divisions of the enemy and his best air force units have already been destroyed and have met their end on the battlefields,

the enemy continues to advance and throw new troops into battle.

"Hitler's forces have succeeded in conquering Lithuania, a considerable part of Latvia, the western part of Belarussia, and part of western Ukraine. The Fascist air force expands the range of its bombers and subjects Murmansk, Orsha, Mogilyow, Smolensk, Kiev, Odesa, and Sevastopol to bombardments. A serious danger hangs over our motherland.

"How could it occur that our illustrious Red Army has surrendered a few towns and regions to the Fascist armies? Are the German-Fascist troops really as invincible as the bragging Fascist propaganda machine is relentlessly broadcasting?

"Of course not! History shows that invincible armies do not exist and have never existed. The army of Napoleon was thought to be invincible and yet it was defeated by respectively Russian, English, and German troops. The German army of Kaiser Wilhelm was also considered invincible during the First Imperial War, yet it was defeated more than once by Russian and Anglo-French troops and ultimately destroyed by Anglo-French armies.

"The same should be said about the present Fascist German army of Hitler."

Stalin goes on and on about how Germany has yet to face any real opposition since it's surprise attack. How Germany has violated the non-aggression pact, and would be branded as the aggressor by the rest of the world. How the people of Russia, Europe, America, and Asia will unite to defeat the fascists. How the Soviet people need to recognize the full scope of the danger that threatens the country.

"Therefore, it means life or death of the Soviet state, life or death of the peoples of the Soviet Union, and it concerns the question whether the Soviet peoples remain free or will be subdued. It is imperative that the Soviet peoples understand this and will not remain careless, that they will pull together and base their work on a new military footing, giving no quarter to the enemy.

Furthermore, it is necessary that there shall be no place in our ranks for lamenters, panic mongers, cowards, and deserters; that our people know no fear in battle, and that they shall participate in our national war of liberation against the Fascist suppressors in a sacrificial spirit."

Stalin goes on about how the main characteristics of the Soviet people must be their courage and gallantry. We must put all our labor and efforts on a military footing. We must rise up and protect our rights and territory against the enemy. Fight until the last drop of blood. Exterminate spies, saboteurs and enemy parachutists.

"Anyone who thwarts the national defense by panicking and cowardice must be brought before a military tribunal immediately, regardless of who or what he is."

In the case of a forced retreat, nothing will be left behind. In occupied areas, the enemy's measures must be made to fail. It is a war of liberation, and Russia will have the backing of European and American people.

"A State Defense Committee has begun its work and calls on the entire population to gather around the party of Lenin and Stalin and around the government to lend unselfish support to the Red Army and to the Red Navy in order to defeat the enemy and achieve victory.

"All our efforts in support of our heroic Red Army and our illustrious Red Navy.

"All efforts by the population for the destruction of the enemy.

"Forward, for our victory!"

CHAPTER 33

8 July, 04:00 — Five days later, an ear-splitting explosion blasts me out of my sleep. My eyes fly open to the sound of machine-gun fire, and I instinctively pull a shaking Ita into my arms.

Boom, boom, BOOM, goes another rally of explosions.

We hug and kiss like it might be for the last time, and I spring to the window. "I don't see anyone. They must not be as close as it sounds."

Ita pulls on a shirt and pants and sticks her feet into her best walking boots. "Rivka! Ira! Get dressed!" she yells.

My brain is going at full speed as I jump into my clothes and follow Ita into the hallway where she opens the doors to the children's rooms. "We have to go. Now."

Ratta-tat-tat-tat. Ka-BOOM.

Rivka screams, and Ira's eyes look like saucers.

Ita runs to the kitchen, opens the pantry, extracts four pre-packed rucksacks, and lays them on the kitchen table.

I open the door. We go down the steps, make sure the coast is clear, and sprint across the street to the warehouse on the property of the store, where Herschel and his family are now living. Before I can knock on the door, Herschel opens it.

"We'll be right there!" he says.

Holding up my thumbs and nodding my head, I run back into the house to my parents' room. I pound on the door. "Mama! Papa! We've gotta go!"

Mama pokes her head out of her bedroom with papa shaking behind her. "We can't go."

"What?! You must! Come on!" I say.

Papa pushes mama aside. "We're too old. We'll slow you down. You'll die too."

Pow, pow, pow, pow, pow.

"Go! Run while you can," papa says.

I'm overwhelmed with emotion, and my eyes flood with tears as mama blows me kiss and then closes the door.

"Mama!" I cry.

Ka-boom! This one is much closer.

I run to the kitchen, where I find Ita, Rivka, and Ira wolfing down bread rolls and juice. Ita sticks a roll in my mouth and hands me a glass of apple cider.

We shoulder our backpacks as I scarf down the roll in two bites and drain the glass.

Two backpacks remain.

"Where are grandma and grandpa?" Rivka asks.

I gave her a blank look and her jaw drops in horror.

Pop, pop, pop, pop, pop, pop, pop.

"Move!" I scream, and we leave the two backpacks behind.

We dart into the street like animals fleeing a forest fire.

A warehouse near the railroad tracks only a few blocks away has been reduced to rubble. The synagogue and several apartment buildings are on fire. Two tanks and a squad of soldiers proceed in our direction.

A tank fires on a brick warehouse across the street. BOOM! A flying rock hits Ita in the face, knocking her to the ground.

"Ita!" I scream, kneeling over her. Red blood pours out of a gash above her left eye. I wrestle a handkerchief out of my back pocket and use it to blot Ita's wound. "Take this and apply pressure," I say.

Boom. Boom. Boom!

She clambers to her feet.

"Come on!" I yell, and as a family we run, carrying only the sacks on our backs.

"What about Hershel and Sarah?" Ita asks.

"They'll catch up. They know where to meet us," I say.

Tata, tat, tat, tat. Bam. Bam. Bam. Boom!

We zigzag through a neighborhood east among the denizens of Kalarash who are in carts, on horseback and on foot. We bump and dodge our way out of the village, toward the horse path to Voinova.

At the northeastern border of Kalarash, we stop for a quick breather as we ponder the path that wends up a hill. We're not the only ones who thought of this route. I watch others heading up the hill.

The sound of gunfire and explosions is almost continuous.

We press on. Ita, Rivka, Ira, and I huff and puff up the hill with every ounce of our strength and determination. The gash above Ita's eye oozes blood.

I count our rhythm, "One, two, three, four. Stay strong," I say. "One, two, three, four. We must keep moving," I say.

We are all relieved when we reach the summit. We pause to catch our breath and let our heartrates slow down.

We look back. Immediately seared into all our memories is the view of Kalarash, our home-shtetl, engulfed in flames.

06:30 — We continue down the hill into the next valley, and I clasp my fingers on the back of my head when at last I catch sight of the Kirilenko's Farm. It's considerably farther than I remember.

We stop as we enter the property. Other groups who took our departure route pass through without slowing down, while everyone remains quiet. Soon, we appear to be the only ones around, at least for the time being. I take a deep breath and scan the property as dim morning light flattens my view, but nothing moves.

Waving to the others to stay behind, I tip-toe up to the main house, sidestep a fresh pile of horse manure, and observe recent cart tracks, horse and human footprints in the dirt road that lead away to the east. I peek into a window.

"Hello?"

No answer.

I climb the front steps and knock on the door.

No answer.

I arch my eyebrows, look back at my family and raise my hands. "No Kirilenkos."

Rivka shrugs.

We walk to the barn. Looking all around it, I peer through a crack in the door. It appears to be empty, so we go inside.

"No Herschel or Sarah," Ita says.

"They'll be here," I say.

Ita forces a smile but says nothing.

I kiss her, then pull away, focus on her face, and grimace. "Ooh, we need to give your, uh, little boo-boo some attention."

"Yikes, let me see," Rivka says, taking her mama by the hand.

I lead Ita across the barn, and we sit down on a bench.

Rivka retrieves a first-aid kit from her rucksack, wets a clean cloth and cleans the blood from around the wound above Ita's left eye. Rivka wrinkles her nose and bares her teeth.

"It probably needs a couple of stitches," I say.

"Ah," Ita says.

"It's still bleeding," I say.

"A nick above my eye isn't going to stop me," Ita says.

"No, I'm not kidding; you've lost a lot of blood," I say. "You brought a sewing kit, right?"

"For darning socks," Ita says.

"Give it to me!" I say.

Rivka digs a needle and some thread out of Ita's rucksack.

"Thread it," I say.

Ita looks on in horror as Rivka obeys, then hands me the needle. Ita grits her teeth and sits in superhuman silence as I bend the needle and then sew up the gash above her eye—three excruciating stitches.

Rivka applies a bandage.

When the spectacle concludes, Ira reclines on a pile of hay and we all join him in silence, breathing heavily. War noises rumble from the other side of the hill.

Rivka begins to cry. "Do you think we'll ever see grandma and grandpa again?"

Ita hugs her. "I don't know, honey." She kisses her on the head. "I don't know."

We. All. Cry.

For an excruciating twenty minutes, I resist the urge to continue.

Ita passes around a canteen of water. I take a few sips and make sure everyone gets some.

"Can I have some sausage?" Ira asks.

"You just ate less than two hours ago," Ita says. "We must save what food we have for later."

06:50 — At last, we hear footsteps outside the barn. I run, peek out and wave my arm out the door. I smile back at Ita and nod my head. "It's Herschel and Sarah!"

There's a flurry of hushed greetings seasoned with relief as everyone greets them.

Hershel gets a panicked look on his face. "Where are mama and papa? I thought they came with you."

I give him a numb stare and shake my head. "They wouldn't come."

"Wouldn't come?!" Sarah shrieks.

"They insisted they'd slow us down," Ita says. "Then I got hit in the face with a piece of flying concrete."

"Oh my God," Sarah says, looking at Ita's bandaged forehead. "Are you okay?"

Rivka and Ita reiterate that segment of the morning's drama.

Herschel and I hug each other and, again, cry in silence as Ita, Sarah, and Rivka group hug.

"Drink some water," Ita says, handing Herschel and Sarah the canteen.

Herschel and Sarah savor a few sips of water, then we sit for some time and let them gather themselves.

We all jump at a fresh round of explosions to the west.

"We need to keep moving," I say.

CHAPTER 34

07:10 — The Gershovich *mishpaha* pushes east.

"We must keep moving," I say, "one, two, three, four."

We see more and more families, groups of people, fleeing east the same as us but we keep our distance. Two, three, four.

As we march on, deep in my soul I miss papa, I yearn for him to tell me what to do, and suddenly it dawns on me.

"Two, three, four."

That I have reluctantly become the family's conductor. Fuck.

I've wanted this for so long, but not like this. Not now. Aches and pains surface all over my body. I favor my right leg and hold my lower back.

Ita frequently staggers like she's drunk and stops.

"I'm okay," she insists. "Keep going."

Rivka clears her throat and sings in a soft voice:

Hava nagila,

Hava nagila,

Hava nagila ve-nismeḥa.

I tear a limb from a birch tree and conduct. Ita and Ira join in, and Rivka dances, spinning in circles.

Hava neranenah,

Hava neranenah,

Hava neranenah ve-nismeḥa.

Soon the entire family is singing.

Uru, uru aḥim!

Uru aḥim be-lev sameaḥ.

Uru aḥim, uru aḥim!

Be-lev sameaḥ.

We quiet down when our paths merge with another party of people headed in the same direction. I smile and bow my head in recognition to the man leading the group, who I've seen in the store. I wave and we let them walk ahead.

We walk all day and all night along what widens from a horse trail to a dirt road that runs along the edge of a forest. We pass Voinova, Codreanca and continue toward Butuceny.

Nobody says anything. We just trudge out of fear, grit, and stubbornness.

9 July, 10:40 — The hum of an engine reverberates through the quiet of the night. I raise my hand, and everybody stops. Ira nearly walks into Rivka's back.

Ita looks at me and lowers her eyebrows. We both squint at the horizon to the east. The noise gets louder. Above the hills, two small dots steadily grow.

I scan our surroundings. It is a good twenty meters to the closest cover, which is the edge of the forest on the other side of a creek.

"You suppose it's one of ours?" Ira asks with irony in his voice. Everyone, exhausted, freezes, staring at the sky.

Quicker than anyone expects, the planes close in on us. We scatter. The hum becomes a roar, and in formation, the planes dive from the sky. ROAAAAAARRRRRR. Tat, tat, tat, tat. The planes pass over, spraying the group with machine-gun fire.

I motion to Ira, grab Rivka, and he and Ita dash across the creek toward the forest line.

"Go!" Herschel yells.

The hum of the engines fade, and just when we think it won't return, it grows louder once again.

Ita, Rivka, Ira and I reach the trees. I look back. Herschel slips while fording the creek. Sarah pauses to help him up.

"Take cover!" I shout. "They're making another pass!"

The two press themselves back against the bank of the ravine as the roar of the Luftwaffe grows loud again. ROaaaAAARRRrrr. Ratta, tat, tat, tat, tat, tat.

The roar of the airplanes fades into the distance.

Herschel and Sarah appear over the bank of the creek. I run out and help them into the cover of the forest.

11:45 — I consider continuing when again we hear the roar of aircraft. We stay under cover of the forest and walk with difficulty over logs and through thickets until we find a flat spot with access to the creek.

Everyone collapses on the ground.

We shed our rucksacks. Rivka pulls an apple from hers and takes a bite.

"Don't eat too much!" Ita says. "We don't know how long this food will last."

We brush the dust off our pants, sit in the grass, eat careful rations of food, and drink some water from the creek.

Within minutes, we all fall asleep from sheer exhaustion.

CHAPTER 35

15:45 — When I wake up, I don't know what day it is, but it's light out and every muscle in my body aches. My mind recounts the events of the day before, I'm about to get up when Rivka sits up and stretches. It brightens my soul that she is alive and well until suddenly she convulses and shrieks, which I quickly figure out is because she has an insect in her hair, which she shakes to the ground and kills.

The commotion wakes up Ita and the rest of the *mishpaha.*

"Are you okay?" Ita whispers.

"Just a bug," Rivka says as she takes a deep breath and pounds the ground with her fist.

Ita and I make eye contact, smile at each other. Again I thank God that we are both alive. Then we hug for a long time, then kiss.

"Good morning," I say, noticing that the bandage over her eye has come loose. In a glance, I examine the wound, which is swollen but doesn't look infected, and press the bandage back onto her forehead.

"Good morning," she replies.

"I love you," I say.

"I love you, too," she says.

We both look over as Rivka groggily stands up, scans the sky, and walks to the creek's edge. She lays down on her stomach on its grassy bank, dunks her face into a clear pool, drinks heartily, washes her hands, then splashes more water on her face.

She rolls over, bending her knees, and stares at the sky as she comes around to consciousness. She drinks again from the creek, stands up, and looks at the bruised and dusty group that is her family, then gets a terrified look on her face.

"Where's my bag?" Rivka says, running back to the campsite in a panic.

"What? What's wrong?" Ita asks.

"Where is my rucksack?" she says, starting to cry.

Ita and I look around. "I don't see it," I say.

"Mine is gone, too," Ira says.

"Oh, my God! So, is mine," Ita says.

I jump up and scan the immediate area and, finding nothing, I kick the dirt.

Herschel and Sarah wake up.

"What? What's happening?" Sarah says.

"Our bags are gone. Somebody must have cleaned us out while we slept," I say.

Herschel and Sarah scramble around in their immediate realm. Nothing.

"No!" Herschel screams.

"Keep it down," I say.

"Everyone is desperate," Ita says.

We all sit in silence and Rivka begins to cry. "No! Please, God! Tell me this isn't happening. Every piece of jewelry, every memento of my former life is... gone." Rivka spreads her fingers and wiggles them as if sand were passing through them.

"We're alive and we have each other," I say.

Rivka sits and cries for a very long time.

20:00 — German aircrafts continue their patrols, so we wait until a blanket of darkness covers central Moldova before I lead my family back onto the road and we resume our easterly trek.

We walk all night.

CHAPTER 36

10 July, 1941, 05:45 — As the sun comes up the next morning, we exhaustedly come upon a small house not far from the road. Smoke billows from the chimney, and we all salivate at the smell of baking bread.

At the same time, Ita and I spot an oblong ornament affixed diagonally to the inside of the door jamb at about head height, inscribed with Hebrew. We look at each other.

"They have a *mezuzah*," I say.

"It used to go without saying that if Jewish people were in a strange city and found themselves in need, if they found another Jewish person or family, they could count on them to be kind and help in any way that they could."

"Let's pray that holds true now," I say as I motion for Herschel, Sarah and the kids to stay back while Ita and I cautiously approach the house. In the least-threatening way I can muster, I rap on the door.

It is some time before a woman, who is probably in her forties but looks much older, opens the door and peeks through a crack. Ita and I smile and wave, coaxing the woman to open the door wider. She has straight, shoulder-length graying hair, a long, bulbous nose, and dark bags under her eyes.

"Hello!" I say in Yiddish. "We mean you no harm. We have been running for three days..." I pause.

The woman's look indicates that she understands, and she understands why.

"And we are tired and hungry. Please help us," I plead.

The woman, who wears a black wool dress with a white apron around her waist, appraises Ita and me. She glances behind us at the rest of our entourage, takes a deep breath, and appears to process an internal dialogue. At last, she cracks a weary smile and says, "My name is Dvore, please come in."

I flash an "okay" sign to the family.

"Thank God," Rivka says. "We may have found the last bastion of human decency on earth."

We file into the small but warm house and are enveloped by the smell of baking bread. In the living room is a couch and enough chairs for everyone.

"Please, take a seat," Dvore says.

I flash a grin Ita, raise my eyebrows and motion for everyone to sit. Everyone collapses into the nearest seat.

"You must be hungry," Dvore says.

"Yes. That bread smells like heaven," I say.

"Your timing is impeccable." The woman smiles and goes into the kitchen. She opens the oven and pulls out a perfectly browned loaf of bread.

"Do you live here alone?" Ita asks.

"No. My husband and son are… gone. To war," she says.

"I'm so sorry," Sarah says. "My two sons are, too."

There was a long silence as the woman cut the bread into slices.

"Can I help you?" Ita asks.

"No, don't worry about me. Relax."

"Where are we?" Ira asks.

"Near Butuceny," Dvore says.

Ira's mouth shifts into the shape of an "O." He extracts a map from his pocket and looks at it. He points toward the middle and says, "That's about eighty kilometers from where we started."

Dvore carries a tray with the sliced loaf of bread and containers of honey and strawberry preserves, sets it before us and then goes back to the kitchen for a pitcher of water and glasses.

Ita makes sure everyone is polite as we make short work of the loaf of bread, washing it down with water. We chat with Dvore, ingratiating ourselves to her with personal family stories.

I muffle a belch and say, "The question is where do we go from here?"

"To sleep," Ira says, barely able to keep his eyes open. Whether in chairs or on the floor, everyone finds an adequate spot and falls asleep.

17:00 — "It's weird. We haven't heard any bombing or planes all day," I say.

"Plug in the radio," Ira says.

"Very funny," Rivka says.

There is a pause in the conversation, and my attention goes to Ita's forehead. "How is your eye feeling?" I ask Ita.

"Much better," she says.

"May I have a look?"

"Sure," she says.

I remove the bandage and examine it. "It looks good."

"We endure what we have to," she says.

"I think these stitches are about ready to come out," I say.

Ita gives me a look of dread.

I hold her hand reassuringly. "I had a similar wound when I was a child, and as I recall, the doctor took the stitches out after about three days. You don't want to leave them in too long."

She closes her eyes and takes a deep breath. "Okay, let's do it."

"Okay."

"Rivka, will you get the scissors for me?" I ask.

Rivka rummages in her rucksack, pulls out the first aid/sewing kit and produces a small pair of scissors and some tweezers.

As everyone watches, I deftly snip and pull out the stitches. Again, Ita doesn't so much as utter a peep as I perform the procedure.

When I finish, Rivka applies a new bandage, and everyone is amazed and relieved.

"You're one tough woman," I say.

Ira changes the subject. "I still want to know what's happening with the Germans."

"It's horrible not knowing anything. There's an invasion one day and then nothing," Ita says.

"Maybe it's over," I say.

"Maybe we just overreacted and everything is going to return to normal, or at least to the way it was," Herschel says.

"It could be that Stalin has negotiated some sort of truce with Germany," Ita adds.

"It could be a lot of things. Maybe I should go back and investigate," I say.

"It would be awful if we continue on when we don't have to," Ita says.

"Okay, okay, let's find out," I say. "I'll go back and check it out. I think it would be best if the rest of you stay here and save your strength."

Dvore says, "You all are welcome to stay here until Elazar returns. Let's hope it will be with good news, and you can all return home."

CHAPTER 37

20:15 — As it begins to get dark, thanks to the generosity of Dvore, I pack a nap sack with some bread, fruit, and vegetables, and she also throws in a knife and some matches. I set off on foot, heading west back toward Kalarash.

My whole body feels sore and tired, but I am motivated by the hope that the engagement with the Germans might have stopped. Without my family, I can make much better time.

About midnight, I spot something that makes my heart race and my tired legs hopeful. On the outskirts of the vacant town of Butuceny, grazing on the side of the road, is a buckskin-colored mare with a black mane and a black tail. Fully saddled and wearing a bridle with the reins dragging on the ground, she doesn't spook as I quietly approach; she just calmly looks at me as she munches on grass.

I scan the area for its owner but seeing no one, I dig part of a carrot out of my bag and offer it to the horse. I glance at the horse's underside and say, "Hello, girl. What's your name?"

She snorts and sniffs the carrot.

"I'm going to call you Ruth," I say, "it means friendship in Hebrew."

I gently put the carrot into the horse's mouth, and as she munches, I notice blood on the cantle and more on the fender. I pet her nose and scratch her between the ears.

"Where's your owner?"

She snorts again—she obviously doesn't speak Yiddish or Hebrew—and I can't believe my good fortune. I look around one more time, then say, "Well, Ruthie, I don't see anybody, so I guess you and I are going to be friends. I'm a tired old man and I could sure use a ride."

I put my foot in the left stirrup, grab the horn, and swing up onto the horse. Mounted, I take the reins in my hands and gently kick the horse. "Let's go, girl."

20:30 — I ride west at a steady trot, not wanting to overwork the horse but hoping to cover as much territory as possible as quickly as possible.

I ride long and hard. It gets to where the pain from each bounce in the saddle is excruciating. Somewhere along the road, in the dark, the horse takes a fork that veers to the south. A few hours later, I enter the small town, which is deserted. Physically unable to go another centimeter, I steal refuge in an abandoned barn and catch a few winks.

CHAPTER 38

11 July, 1941, 05:23 — Just as the sun is coming up, my eyes open as I realize today is my fifteenth wedding anniversary, and then I hear gunfire.

I peek out of the barn, see what I surmise is a German patrol maybe 100 meters away, then hear more gunfire. Tat, tat, tat. Then silence. I look again. The patrol moves away from me and out of my field of vision.

I look west. I'm not sure where I am, but from my map, I'm guessing the village of Peresecina. If I'm right, Kalarash is still at least fifty kilometers away. To the south, there is a red glow on the horizon, and a blackish haze that smells and tastes of smoke makes my lungs feel raspy.

Movement catches my eye, and I quickly hide when I hear a female voice speak in Russian. A group of men and women on foot approach wearing white-cotton shirts and black vests—Bessarabian peasants, I presume.

As they get closer, I can tell for sure that they're refugees like me, so I muster the nerve to come out of my cover and raise my hand in a peaceful gesture. They are startled initially, whisper, and then cautiously wave back as they approach.

"Where are you going?" says a man in his mid-thirties with red hair and a red mustache. The others in his group, clearly exhausted and scared, look at me suspiciously.

"Back to Kalarash to see if the attack is over and maybe it will be safe to return," I say.

The redhead glares grimly. "No. Not in your wildest dreams." He points south. "See that smoke? That's Kishinev. The Germans have bombed it heavily. It's on fire, and they have taken over. There is a patrol here now."

"I saw them," I say.

"They are killing anyone who hasn't left," the man says. "I'm telling you, there is nothing in Kalarash."

"Are you sure? They attacked and now days have gone by, and I haven't heard anything."

Pop! Pop! Tat, tat, tat. We all flinch and take cover at the sound of gunfire.

"Until I saw that patrol this morning," I say.

The redhead scrunches up his face and nods. "Right now, the Germans are kicking our asses, so if you want to live, you'd better flee east now, while you have time. They're here, there are a lot more coming, and there is no sign of anyone stopping them."

I split with the peasants as they head north looking for family members. I still hear the gunfire of the German patrol and the roar of planes.

Rather than risk traveling on the road by day, I comb the outskirts of Peresecina for a place to hide. That's when I spot a *podval* behind a deserted farmhouse.

To my delight, I climb down the ladder into the cool hole to behold rows of glass jars. I struggle to open one, but it won't budge. I pull out the knife that Dvore gave me, tap the lid several times, then try again. The jar opens, releasing the sweet scent of strawberry preserves. I tilt it into my mouth and devour half its contents on the spot.

I find pickles, beets and peaches, and an array of other preserves. I take out the bits of bread I brought from Dvore's and eat to my heart's content.

Making sure the hatch on the *podval* is secure, I stretch out on the cool dirt and fall into a deep sleep. It's well after noon before I wake up.

When darkness returns, I load up as much food as I can and head back to find my family.

CHAPTER 39

12 July, 1941, 07:00 — Much sooner than I expect, I clop up to Dvore's house. Ita runs out as I approach, and I jump off the horse and hug and kiss her. She has removed her bandage, and while the bruising is getting worse, the wound is healing.

Ita pats the animal on the nose and says, "Nice horse."

"I got her just for you! Happy belated anniversary," I say.

"Thank you. I almost forgot, too. Where'd you get her?"

"She found me. Thank God! I have no idea what happened to her previous owner." I clear my throat. "There was some blood on the saddle. Anyway, I've named her Ruth, and look at this."

I unlash a bag from the horse's saddle and show Ita its contents.

"This is fantastic!" she says, but then her elation turns back to concern. "But you're back so soon. What's the verdict on Kalarash?"

As Rivka comes out of the house, I shake my head grimly and say, "It's way worse than we imagined. I didn't go all the way, but I saw enough to know for sure that there is no Kalarash. Kishinev is on fire, and the Germans are on the move."

Rivka bursts into tears. "Poor grandma and grandpa. I miss them so much."

Ita hugs Rivka.

Dvore came out on her porch and admires the horse. "She's a beauty," she says.

Herschel limps up and says, "It's a pity we don't have five or six more."

Dvore rubs her chin and says, "I might be able to help you out."

"Do you know where we can get more horses?" Herschel asks.

"No. But my neighbors are gone, and… follow me. Bring the horse." She walks toward a farmhouse, a barn and two other small shacks that are about 100 meters away across a field.

Ira mounts the horse, and Herschel and I lead it after Dvore around the far side of the barn, where Ira's eyes light up when we see a cart built for hauling produce. Ira jumps off the horse and climbs aboard the cart.

"This isn't bad at all," Ira exclaims.

I scrutinize the contraption, taking a mental inventory of every element of the carriage I can see. There are two seats in the front of a four-by-six-meter box. "Seems to be in decent repair," I say.

"I don't see any cracks or other debilitating damage," Herschel says as we inspect the wooden chassis and the four wooden-spoked wheels and axels on which it sits.

Inside the barn, Herschel and I manage to pull together various harnesses and leather straps and attach the cart to the horse.

"We've got wheels!" Ira says.

CHAPTER 40

12 July, 1941, 21:00 — "Come with us," Rivka begs Dvore as darkness falls on Buteceny.

"No, I just can't. I'm staying here and that's that. This is all I have, and I don't have the energy to run."

I can't quit thinking about the certain fate of my parents. I know it's on everyone else's mind, but we keep it to ourselves.

"Thank you so much for everything you have done," I say.

Ita gives Dvore a hug and says, "We can't tell you how much we appreciate your extraordinary kindness. We will be eternally grateful."

Fighting tears, Rivka embraces Dvore. "I'll never forget you."

Herschel and Sarah hug her and express their gratitude. Ira waves and she pats him on the head.

With sore feet and heavy hearts, we set off east into the darkness toward Dubossary. Herschel drives the carriage. Sarah sits beside him. Rivka and Ira ride in the back of the cart, and for now Ita and I walk alongside it.

The ride is very bumpy, and it isn't long before Rivka jumps out and walks.

22:00 — Early on, there were relatively few other people, but now, my family can't avoid walking with a growing group of refugees.

"Ugh, all these people," Rivka says.

"I wish they'd walk somewhere else," Ira adds.

I put my arm around Ira. "Everyone is headed in the same direction, we're all in the same predicament, so just keep walking and mind your own business."

I conduct. One foot in front of the other, one, two, three, four, clop-by-clippity-clop, one, two, three, four, we must push on. All. Night. Lo-ong.

CHAPTER 41

13 July, 1941, 06:30 — The road takes us and the growing group of refugees down a hill into a green valley, where we cross a fertile floodplain and come to a wide river.

I squint to try to make out the details on the distant shore and say, "This must be the Dniester River."

Ira looks at his map. "The city on the other side would have to be Dubossary. Maybe we can catch a train there?"

"First we have to get across," Rivka says.

As the sun comes up, the growing group takes a breather in a grove of trees. Some bathe or swim in the river while we all contemplate how to get across.

It's not long before a posse of locals comes through and leads us about a kilometer south to where there is a dock and a barge crossing and, as fate would have it, a barge is coming from the other side just as our group approaches.

After it's secured to the dock, the man who was operating the barge steps onto the dock and waves his hands. "Welcome! I've been authorized by the Soviet Government to transport any and all war refugees."

Relieved, my family and I—forced to be a little pushy—maneuver our way to the front of the line and load our horse, buggy and the whole family on the barge for its first trip across.

"Excuse me, you say the government was expecting us? Did they give you any indication on where we should go from here? Can we catch a train in Dubasari?" I ask.

"I'm afraid not. At this point, there is no train line through Dubasari," the barge operator says.

Rivka slumps in disappointment. Ira groans.

"The closest station to catch a train east is Kotovsk," the operator says.

"Where is that?" Rivka asks.

He points. "It's about seventy-five kilometers northeast. Just follow the road."

"Ugh," Ira says.

After disembarking from the barge, we push on through Dubasari and into the countryside, where there are rows of corn as far as we can see. There has been considerable rain this summer, and the cornstalks are taller than a person, bushy and tasseling.

After the sun rises into the sky, again we hear the roar of German planes. We look around, but there is no barn, grove, or other places to hide.

With no other choice, we all hide amongst the corn for the rest of the day, resting up for the next leg of their journey.

"Thank God the corn is nearly ready to harvest," Rivka says as she gnaws on a raw ear, picking the kernels from between her teeth.

10:15 — When darkness falls, we continue, taking turns riding on the cart throughout night.

We follow the road and pray that in the dark we don't miss a turn or take a wrong one, and that we will still end up in Kotovsk.

When it gets light, it isn't long before we hear the roar of planes overhead, so again we hide from the air patrol in a cornfield.

For two more days we repeat this, making sure to travel in a north-easterly direction.

Always hungry, Rivka and Ira compete to see who can be the first to spot apple trees or any other food that can be foraged.

CHAPTER 42

16 July, 1941, 08:00 — Just when I think I can't take even one more step, we come to the southern outskirts of Kotovsk. I squeeze Ita's hand and feel an excitement that perhaps the endless walking part of our ordeal is coming to an end.

My excitement builds when we cross a railroad track and follow the flow of humanity up Shevchenka Boulevard, which runs parallel to the railroad track and takes us north through the Ukrainian town past two-story stucco apartment buildings not unlike the one we used to own in Kalarash.

As we near the downtown area, I notice that many of the municipal buildings are built in Neo-Gothic and French Neo-classical style.

From about two blocks away, I spot a two-story building with an arch above the entrance to the train station. It is absolutely mobbed with people, and there are no trains in sight.

09:15 — I park the horse and cart under a shady tree, make sure everyone is reasonably well situated, then say, "Sit tight here. I'll go see if I can find out when we can get on the next train."

I step over people sleeping on the sidewalk and fight my way through a throng of humans, the strong scent of body odor, urine, and feces, to push, shove, and wait in line until I finally encounter a uniformed train official.

"Excuse me! Is it possible that we can get on a train to anywhere that will be safe?" I ask.

A very tired looking Ukrainian man with gray hair gives me a blank look, waves his arm at all the people behind me, and says, "You're all in the same predicament."

I question the Ukrainian further, and I then I return to my family.

Ita greets me with a relieved hug and kiss. "Well?"

"Do you want the good news first? Or the bad news?" I ask.

"The good news!" Rivka says.

"The good news is there will be a train. And… remember the last year of turning over all our gross receipts to the Soviet Government? That will pay for our ticket."

Ira gives me a glum stare. "What's the bad news?"

"The next train isn't for two days," I say.

"What?! The Germans could be here by then."

"Maybe. But then again, maybe they won't. We have no other choice."

We set up camp as refugees continue to flood into Kotovsk. The spot where I parked our cart becomes our territory that we must defend.

I disconnect the horse from the cart and wish I had a brush for her coat. Ita and I leave the kids with Herschel and Sarah and walk the horse down to the river where we bathe, wash Ita's eye, and let Ruth have a nice drink and graze on the banks.

"There sure are a lot of people waiting for the same train," Ita says.

"And they all stink," I say, scrubbing my body with no soap.

"I can't take this! I just want to go home and have my life back," Ita says.

"It might be a long time before that happens, so get used to it," I say.

"Nothing like walking forever in the middle of the night and sleeping on the sidewalk in front of a train station to make you appreciate what you had," she says.

"At least we have each other," I say as I put my arm around her.

"How would you like to be alone right now?"

"I wouldn't. I couldn't take it. Your eye is looking much better," I say.

"You did a good job sewing it up. Thanks."

"You're welcome."

"Now I'm worried about getting on that train," Ita says. "How do they determine who gets on first? Will there be seats?"

"I don't know," I say.

"If we don't get on, when is the next one? What if the Germans come?"

"Ita! We'll be okay."

17 July, 1941 — After a miserable night not sleeping among the unwashed masses, we wait all day, fearing the arrival of more German planes, sitting on the cart, watching more and more exhausted, filthy, injured and otherwise rattled people arrive.

We take turns riding the horse to the river for a drink and to graze.

Returning from one such trip, Ita asks, "What are we going to do with Ruthie—and the cart—when we get on the train?"

"I don't know. I'll sell them if I can, but I'm hesitant to give them up until I'm sure that we will, in fact, be getting on the train," I say.

"Do you seriously think we can get any money for them?" Ita asks.

"If not, I guess if we just leave her..." I begin.

"The next person who needs them will pick up where we left off," Ita finishes.

CHAPTER 43

18 July, 1941, 05:00 - I wake up and immediately, my brain begins pre-meditating the day ahead.

After an hour or so, Ita wakes up next to me, and as always, we hug and kiss good morning.

As the rest of the family comes around, Ita makes sure everyone gets some food in their stomachs and packs what few belongings we have.

8:45 — The whole town is abuzz when we hear a train rolling into the outskirts of Kotovsk.

At that moment, I hug Ruth good-by, untie her from the cart, and set her free.

With me in front, my family makes a human wedge and begins plowing our way toward the boarding platform to get as close as possible to the front of the line as the train rolls into the station.

Ita and the kids cringe as some people give us dirty looks, but I press ahead and whisper to Ita, "Nice guys finish last."

Not everyone is as organized, so as a result, we end up in a pretty good position.

It's not long before the conductors open the gates and I make sure my whole family stays together and gets on the same car.

I smell horse manure when the conductor slides the door open to the car in which God or fate has determined we will ride out of Kotovsk. I look in and see some straw on a wooden floor, but no seats and no windows. "Quickly!" I say, motioning my family toward the front of the car.

People cram in ahead of us, but we manage to stake out enough space for us all to sit on the floor in the front right corner of the car. I'm relieved that we have two walls to separate us from the rest of the throng and that we are upwind—at least from the people in our car.

"Moo!" Ira says as nearly fifty people cram into the car behind us.

Rivka elbows him and gives him a dirty look.

Gingerly sitting down on the wooden floor, Sarah says, "At least we don't have to walk."

"I'll second that," Herschel says, as he and Sarah plop down on the floor.

Rivka leans her back against the side of the car. A fly buzzes her face, lands on her thigh, and she expertly swats it with her hand and kills it. She cranes her head around and peeks through a crack between two slats.

CHAPTER 44

10:15 — The train chugs out of Kotovsk. "Where are we headed?" Rivka asks.

"Dnepropetrovsk," I say.

"Where?" Rivka smiles sarcastically and elbows Ira. "Why can't we go someplace pronounceable?"

"What's it called?" Ira says.

"Dne-pro-pe-trovsk," I enunciate. "Work on it."

"See if you can get it memorized before we get there," Rivka quips.

For hours upon hours we ride on the floor of the cattle car as the train endlessly vibrates down the track.

Rivka peeks through her crack in the car and watches the countryside speed by.

"I spy something blue," Rivka says.

Ira looks around the car, elbows her and points at an old woman wearing a blue head scarf.

"Wrong."

Ira frowns. It's gets hotter as the day progresses, and somebody manages to get the door to the car open for some fresh air. Ira looks at a small village as it whizzes by and asks, "Animal, vegetable or mineral?"

"Mineral," Rivka says.

He looks again, pans his gaze over the rest of the passengers and asks, "Inside the car or out?"

"Out." Rivka sits expressionless.

"The sky?"

Rivka smiles and nods. "Your turn."

Hours tick by agonizingly slow, and nobody says anything.

The sun goes down, and slowly darkness descends.

I manage to fall sleep, but it seems like moments later that I wake up hungry.

Ita rations dry bread and apples she has hoarded along the way to Kotovsk.

Ira sits repeating to himself, working on his pronunciation: "Dne-pro-pe-trovsk. Dne-pro-pe-trovsk."

More than once, Rivka looks on in revulsion as Ira dry heaves from motion sickness.

CHAPTER 45

19 July, 1941, 05:30 — Just as it's beginning to get light, I wake up and peek through the crack in the railroad car. The countryside is lush and green, and a herd of brown cows wade amongst lily-pads in a creeping brown river about 100 meters across.

The train follows the river for some time until the rural agricultural land is increasingly developed with houses, then rows of houses, then taller apartment and office buildings. On the far bank of the river gleams an edifice with multiple, gilded-onion domes adorning the roof.

I point through the crack and say to Ita, "Look! Wow!"

I get out of the way, and Ita crawls over and squints through the crack. "It must be a Christian church or a monastery. You're right, that's beautiful."

"Lemme see!" Ira shoves his way to the crack. Rivka patiently waits her turn.

People in the rest of the car overhear Ira, and everyone tries to get a glimpse. I feel an excitement in the air. My butt aches, my elbows have bruises from resting on the wooden floor, and I yearn to jump up and down.

"Is this it, Mama? Is this where we're going to stay?" Ira asks.

Ita and I exchange hopeful glances. Ita shrugs. "Hard to say."

"Doesn't look like a bad place. Wow! It looks like Paris," Ira says.

Rivka peeks out again. "It does not."

Ira squints. "You don't know what Paris looks like."

"I will."

Ita smooths Rivka's coarse hair. "Yes, you will, baby," she says.

Herschel takes a turn peeking through the crack. "Wow! That's a big city. Some of the buildings look like they could be in Paris."

We all gather what belongings we have from Dvore and what we have foraged since we were robbed the first night. Ita puts a tin cup, a spoon and small plate into her bag, then takes a broken brush and pulls it through her hair.

There is a rise in the noise level in the car as the other passengers begin to fuss, preparing to disembark.

The train crosses the Dniepr River over a long trestle bridge. There is a flutter of wings as a flock of geese takes off. A fishing boat bobs across the wake of a larger vessel.

Everyone in the car leans to the right as the train takes a left turn and runs parallel to a busy boulevard.

Two or three tense minutes later, Ira pushes Rivka aside and looks through the crack as the train pushes into a long, covered platform in front of a three-story white building that frames a glass atrium in the middle. Across the top of the right side, in big white letters, it says, "Dnepropetrovsk."

"Dne-pro-pe-trovsk," Ira enunciates perfectly.

Rivka looks out and sees the same sign. "Very good."

Ira sticks his tongue out at Rivka as the train comes to a screeching halt. Everyone gets to their feet and presses toward the door.

"Okay, okay! Easy everybody," I yell. "Take your time so nobody gets hurt."

Rivka and Ira jump out. They carefully help Ita and I, as well as Herschel and Sarah, get off the cattle car.

Rivka reads signs around the station. "Turns out the city is actually call Dniepr."

"Is this where we will spend the war?" Ira asks.

"I don't know," I answer. "Right now, we need to worry about where we will sleep tonight."

With the sea of refugees, we pour out of the train station. With no money and no friends in town to call upon, we set up camp on the sidewalk next to a big white building.

The cement is cold and hard, and we are all awake much of the night.

I pray that we will hear that the war is over.

"Do you think we're far enough away from the Germans?" Rivka asks.

"I don't know."

"When can we get on another train?" Ira asks.

"I don't know."

The next morning, after a scant breakfast, I put on my hat and stand up. "If we're going to stay here, I've got to find work."

"*We* need to find work," Herschel says.

"And we need a place to stay," I say.

Ita and Sarah clean up the mess from our breakfast

rations. "Let's hope we don't have to spend too many nights camping in front of the train station," Ita says.

"Please, God," Sarah says.

"We'll see if we can apply for *kartochky*," Herschel says.

Herschel and I kiss our wives, wave to Rivka and Ira, and set off into the city.

With each day that passes, we all get more daring as we explore Dniepr.

Ita, Rivka, Ira, and I walk down a green pedestrian boulevard called Yarvonytscy Avenue. "Yar-vo-NYT-sky," Ira repeats.

A tram passes by on tracks powered by overhead wires.

A bellman turns us away when we try to enter the Grand Hotel Ukraina.

We visit the campus of the National Mining University, which Rivka reads was founded during the reign of Nicholas II in 1899.

We walk by a white church with a large, gilded-onion dome cupola, and three smaller gilded-onion domes on the roof. In front is a sign that says: Bryansk Church, House of Organ and Chamber Music.

We stroll along the deep Dniepr river and watch large freight boats float by.

8 August, 1941, 15:00 — Rivka, Ita, and Sarah return from bathing in the river.

Rivka shudders in revulsion as we push through the crowd of refugees sit down on the sidewalk inside our square of declared space.

"Bad news," Ita says.

"What?" I ask.

"As we were bathing in the river, I noticed that Rivka was scratching her head. So… I inspected her scalp, and sure enough, she has lice," Ita says.

"Great," I say. "What next?"

"We then checked each other," Sarah adds, "and we all have them, so you guys probably do, too."

"I suppose it was only a matter of time," I say.

"I miss my bed in Kalarash," Rivka says. "If this stupid war hadn't started, at this moment I would be in choir class. I don't want to sleep another night on the sidewalk!"

We hear the roar of a plane.

Minutes later, BOOOM! A bomb hits the train station a hundred meters from us. The ground shakes. A huge chunk of the building tumbles down from the corner of the roof.

The bombing continues much of the afternoon. By the grace of God, we don't get hit.

The noise quiets down when it gets dark.

I wake up every hour or so all night to the sound of a baby crying two campsites over.

CHAPTER 46

10 August, 1941, 09:00 — Sweltering in the summer heat, my family and I stand squished in a mob—spreading lice—pushing and shoving to get on a train out of Dniepr.

"Where is this train headed?" Rivka asks.

"East," Ira says, pointing toward the front of the train and the rising sun.

"Khasavyurt," I say. "That's what somebody said."

"Wherever that is," Ira says. "We don't have to somehow get tickets?"

"It is war," I say, "nobody has any money. It's communism."

We push and flow with the crowd, expecting to be boarding another cattle train, but when we get inside, Rivka's mouth drops open when there's an aisle down the middle of the car and actual rows of wooden seats on either side. Even more astonishing is there's a door with a sign on it that says, "Toilet." She looks at Ira in disbelief.

"Woah, this is luxurious," Ira says.

The push-and-shove lands the six of us in two rows of seats on the right side of the train near the front of the car.

We wait for nearly an hour as the rest of the people fight to pack the train.

As the train heads southeast out of Dniepr, a uniformed Russian in his thirties pushes a cart into the aisle next to us. He's blonde and has no facial hair. "Is anybody hungry?"

Nearly floored with disbelief, we all emphatically nod our heads and in unison say, "Yes!"

The conductor gives us each a paper bag, as he does with everyone on the car. I tear into mine and find a piece of bread that is soft, isn't moldy and smells fresh. There's also a hunk of dry sausage, feta cheese wrapped in paper, a slice of cucumber, and an apple.

We all stop talking, and all I hear is munching and happy, satisfied sighs.

Outside of Donetsk the conductor comes back through. To our astonishment, this time he passes out clothing, which is mostly blue shirts and black pants, and he does an amazing job of getting us the sizes that fit us. At first, we think we'll take turns going to the restroom to change, but everyone on the car has the same idea, so we put modesty aside—as if we hadn't left it on the sidewalk in Kotovsk—and change right where we are. We would kill to have a bath first, but it feels great to have on clean clothes.

11 August 1941 — After about twenty-two hours, we make a stop in Rostov on Don. Rivka barely bothers to look out the window.

The train continues southeast across rolling hills—mostly agricultural land with the Caucus Mountains to the south. We pass through Zemograd, Tselina, Salsk, Arzgir, Kochubey and Babayurt.

We travel for another brutal day and night, covering nearly 1,300 kilometers, until the train stops in Khasavyurt.

"Kha-sa-VYURT. Can you say that, Ira?" Rivka asks.

«Kha-sa-VYURT.»

CHAPTER 47

The third day in Khasavyurt, another miracle even more amazing than being hungry and then being fed on the train occurs. Military trucks arrive to distribute tents to all the refugees. We even get two—one for Ita, myself and the kids, and one for Herschel and Sarah.

We stake out plots next to each other in a park across from the train station and settle into what seems like luxury.

"At last, we are not sleeping under the stars!" Rivka says.

We decorate our tents, and in addition to the immeasurable improvement to our sleeping accommodations, the military also help us, at last, with food rations.

Life is the best it has been since we left Kalarash, but almost precisely two weeks into our stay in Khasavyurt, in the distance, again we hear the roar of planes.

Trembling, Ita and Rivka hug me.

"Not again," Rivka says.

Boom! Boom, boom, BOOOOOOOM!

5 September, 1941 — We pack up our tents and all our gear, as it is, and out of Khasavyurt we catch a train headed southeast.

"I think this is train 'C', that connects in Makhachkala," I say.

"I'm not going to bother learning how to pronounce that one," Rivka says as the train passes an oil refinery.

We continue south for ten hours through agricultural planes and arid landscapes. The Caucus Mountains grow increasingly closer off the right side of the train. To the left are the sandy beaches and sometimes the rocky shores of the Caspian Sea.

Electrical wires parallel to the tracks look like spider webs. Clusters of wooden oil derricks and pumpjacks are ubiquitous, bobbing their heads like nodding horses.

7 September, 1941 — The train glides into a large, flat metropolis built on the southern shore of a claw-shaped peninsula that jabs into the Caspian Sea.

As the city becomes denser, the train veers away from the coastline and takes a serpiginous route into the city.

A sign whizzes by that says, "Baku."

"It's the capital of Azerbaijan," Ita says.

"Bah-KOO," Rivka says. "That I can pronounce. Try it, Ira."

Ira lowers his eyebrows and frowns at her.

"Mama, where are we going to stay in Baku?" Rivka says with melodramatic irony.

Ita blots her sweaty forehead with her sleeve, gives her a grievous, apologetic look and sighs.

"No, wait, let me guess," Rivka says. "We have a luxurious spot reserved on the ground in a park across from the Baku Train Station."

"At least we have tents," Ita says.

"And hopefully more military food rations," I say.

Within a couple of hours, sure enough, we corner off a camping space and pitch our tents on a patch of dirt in a park across the street from the Baku Railway Station.

"How long you suppose we'll be here?" Ira asks.

"No idea," I say.

The next day, there are no signs of German aircraft, so I flash a determined look at Herschel. "This could be the place," I say.

"Let's go try to find work and a real place to live," Herschel says.

"And better food," Ita says.

We kiss our wives, wave at Rivka and Ira, and set off into Baku.

15 September, 1941 — Ita, Rivka, Ira, and I stand in silence for a long time admiring a landscape by Johann Heinrich Roos in a salon in the new National Art Museum of Azerbaijan, which was recently founded in 1936.

The museum is built in a Baroque-style, De Bour mansion built at the end of the 19th century in the center of Baku, not far from the Fountains Square.

Rivka reads a placard next to the painting, "Roos specialized in pastoral idylls, idealized landscapes with ancient ruins. These pastoral scenes represent the longing of Roos for harmony between men and animals with nature." She looks at Ita. "I have the same longing."

Ita hugs Rivka with one arm and says, "It is so nice to be here with you."

"It's not the Louvre," Rivka says, looks at Ita for a long time in silence, then adds, "But for the first time in a long time, I feel like a cultured human being."

"Look at Roos' brushwork; his use of light and color," Ita says.

Rivka moves her attention to another landscape. She looks at the signature. "Louis Victor Watelin." She takes a deep breath. Next, she looks at a picture of a road winding through the woods by Ivan Shishkin. Beyond that she falls in love with a landscape by Gaspard Dughet.

"When we get settled..." Rivka says.

"Shh. Let's just take it one day at a time, baby," Ita says.

22 September, 1941 - On a chilly fall morning, we hear the roaring of planes.

Angry tears fill Rivka's eyes. She punches Ira in the arm. "Not again. I like Baku."

Hours later, we board a ferry boat headed east across the Caspian Sea.

German planes make a roaring noise, followed by explosions.

Our boat nearly gets hit as it pulls away from Baku. Spray from one of the explosions splashes Rivka in the face.

"Looks to me like they're focusing their bombing on the port and the oil refineries," I say.

The boat sails across the Caspian Sea for thirty-seven hours.

CHAPTER 48

23 September, 1941 — My legs are wobbly when we disembark from the ferry boat in Krasnovodsk, Turkmenistan, where again we set up camp.

2 October, 1941 — We hear planes again and get on yet another southeast-bound train, this one painfully inching across the Turkmenistani Desert.

I gaze out the window at a rolling, pinkish-brown desert, endless kilometers of dirt marbled with white sand and the occasional ridge of dark-brown rock. I knock my head on the window. "There is nothing growing. Nothing living."

For two more days the train wends east and then northeast, farther into the lifeless desert.

CHAPTER 49

3 October 1941, 15:00 — The countryside grows greener as we ride past farmers cultivating fields. The train pushes into residential areas and turns right as it penetrates the center of Kattakurgan, Uzbekistan.

The six of us get off the train with thousands of other refugees into a long, brown train station within which the platforms are not covered. We climb off the train into a dusty cinder-block warehouse with a pitched roof that passes as a train terminal.

We flow into a fetid sea of tired, starving, sick, destitute people.

"By my calculations, we're approximately 3,200 kilometers from Kalarash," Ira says.

Rivka's eyelids droop.

The stream of humanity pushes us a block east of the station to a city park that encompasses a wooden rectangle that extends four square blocks.

I find a nice, flat spot under a tree and put down my bag. There are no rocks, so I use my boot to scratch marks in the dirt to delineate the boundaries of our campsite, where Herschel and I pitch our tents.

Rivka, meanwhile, sits down in the dirt, crosses her legs, sticks out her lower lip, and blows her hair out of her face. A fly lands on her face, but she makes no attempt to show it. "I feel like a fly. My life is worthless. The Germans might as well just swat me dead," she says.

30 October, 1941 — A hospital stands across the street from our camp in Kattakurgan.

We grow accustomed to a pattern. A train rolls into the station, and military medical personnel assist, carry, or wheel wounded soldiers in by the trainload.

Some have bloody bandages wrapped around their heads. Others have wounds to the torso. Many are missing limbs.

"It's a river of blood," Rivka says.

Herschel and I sign up for *kartochki*—food stamps—and put our names on a list for government housing as we explore Kattakurgan. We talk to various social workers, soldiers, and residents of the city. We kill a chicken, raid an apple tree, and proudly bring back food for Ita and Sarah to prepare.

"What did you learn about the city?" Ita asks.

"It is a working-class city in the Samarquand Oblast of the Uzbek Soviet Socialist Republic. It was started in the 18th century as a center of trade and handicrafts," I say.

"It has several light industrial plants that make farm equipment," Herschel reports.

"Now, the Soviets are converting the two biggest manufacturing facilities to aid in the war effort. Both plants will run twenty-four hours a day."

"One is being converted to manufacture parts for tanks, and the other to make ammunition."

As nearly everyone has lice, the city of Kattakurgan sets up a series of fires and giant pots outside the banya, in which we boil our lice-infested clothes and then hang them in the sun to dry. Meanwhile, we bathe in the banya and use fine-toothed combs to—after multiple attempts—finally rid ourselves of the dreadful parasites.

CHAPTER 50

December 1941 – A month and a half later, Herschel and I return to the campsite wearing huge grins. I wave a key. "You're not going to believe this! We're no longer homeless!"

"They issued us two apartments in the same building," Herschel says, also waving a key.

"One for the four of us," I say.

"The other for us," Herschel says, hugging Sarah.

"Thank God! That is amazing news," Ita says.

Rivka jumps to her feet with a slack jaw. "No way."

"Pack it up," I say.

We tear down our tents, collect what few possessions we have from our campsite, and ride a trolly bus far from the center of the city. It takes about fifteen minutes, past eight stops.

We get off the trolley and follow the directions we received to an off-white five-story apartment building. "What kind of architecture would you call that?" Rivka asks.

Ita ignores her and starts climbing stairs. On the fourth floor, we walk down a hall, I stick my key into the door Number 457, swing it open and say, "Welcome home!"

We walk into a starkly furnished apartment that consists of two small bedrooms with a double bed in one and two singles in the other.

Rivka looks at Ira. "What's the name of this town again?"

"Kattakurgan."

"Kat-a-kur-gan," Rivka repeats.

Hershel and Sarah receive a similar apartment next door. There is a small kitchen, which our two families share with two other families. All four families share a single toilet.

Once a week, we go to the *banya*, which is three stops away on the trolly bus.

The women go in the women's side, and Herschel, Ira and I go in on the men's side. We take long, hot showers, and luxuriate in the steam room. We boil our clothes and use fine-toothed combs to remove the lice, but no sooner do we think we're rid of them than they're back.

It becomes mundane.

Most days, Ita fixes lunch at the apartment for Rivka and Ira. She and Sarah make sure we all have dinner together on Friday nights.

"I miss Kalarash! How much can one human being take? To think that I used to complain about my hectic schedule at school. Or about having to learn Russian," Rivka says.

From radio broadcasts and the minimal media coverage, the war sounds terrible.

I get a job as a guard at the ammunition factory. Every day for what seems like an eternity, I show up on time and I wait anxiously for the roar of German planes, but the skies remain quiet.

Every time I get paid, I put a portion of the money in a cavity behind a wall panel in my closet.

Lacking my violin, there is no music in our lives. My soul feels empty.

CHAPTER 51

10 September, 1943 - I get a terrible headache. Body lice have been back for some time, but I don't associate them with the headache.

Pretty much everyone in Kattakurgan constantly battles lice.

"Are you okay?" Ita asks as she touches my forehead. "You feel hot."

In the coming weeks, the headaches come and go.

Ira develops the same symptoms.

Ita is next, displaying the same early symptoms, but then a rash spreads across her body.

Rivka finally gets it too.

"We must see a doctor," Ita says.

"I don't want to go anywhere near that hospital," I say.

We finally go.

We wait for more than a day to see the doctor. When at last we are examined, the doctor says, "You have Typhus."

We all receive medical treatment and spend three weeks in the hospital—in-treatment and de-lousing—before we are released.

Four days later, I hear Ita cough. She coughs again. The lice are back, and her coughing fits get longer and more severe.

"Are you okay?" Rivka asks.

"I don't know. I think it's coming back. My head is pounding something awful," Ita says.

I take Ita back to the hospital.

Between Rivka, Ira and I, someone visits her several times a day. I notice the rash on her chest is becoming more severe.

"I hurt all over. I'm cold," she says.

A doctor comes in and gets a concerned look on his face after he checks her blood pressure. "It's low."

Ita squints even in dim light.

CHAPTER 52

2 December, 1943 — On a clear and cold day, I sit holding Ita's hand as she sleeps, and gently touch the now barely visible scar above her eye. It seems like it's been an eternity since the day we fled Kalarash.

Suddenly, Ita abruptly wakes up and flinches at the sight of me, and, as if seeing me for the first time, she says, "I'm Ita."

I can almost hear the music from Leo's wedding, the moment we met, and I say, "EEE-tah? Ita."

"Yes."

"What a beautiful name. It's so nice to meet you," I say.

"Likewise," she says.

I look at her up close, and in my mind the pieces of our life flashes. Yet unlike the moment I first beheld her, I now fully reconcile my life spent with this angelic voice, this curvy physique, these statuesque features, this woman of my dreams, the love of my life, this sleek, classy goddess in front of me.

"You can really move," she says.

"So can you! No choreographer necessary," I say.

I will the band to play another song, so I might swoop her back onto the dance floor. "Do you want to dance with me?" I say as I brush a tangled lock of hair off her fevered forehead.

Ita laughs. "Always and forever."

Tears come to my eyes. "I'm the luckiest person."

"No, I am. I have you as my loving husband, and two beautiful children."

"We've had some great years," I say.

"Kalarash wasn't so bad," she says.

"And here we are, twenty-one years since we met, in beautiful Kattakurgan," I say.

Her eyes widen. "This isn't Paris?"

"Of course, it is," I say. "We're just off the Champs-Élysées. You've been painting all day."

"Now we're eating in a sidewalk café?" she asks.

Tears stream down my cheeks.

"It's okay," Ita says, then squeezes my hand. A faint smile comes over her face… then she fades out again as abruptly as she'd woken up.

I sit with her for another hour as she drifts in and out of sleep. Suddenly, she opens her blood-shot eyes and says, "Take care of Rivka and Ira."

"What do you mean? You're going to be okay," I say.

Ita shakes her head and grimaces.

"No! Ita don't leave me," I say. "I don't want to live without you. I need you."

Ita squeezes my hand, and then she goes limp.

"No! Doctor, somebody! Help!"

A nurse rushes in and looks at Ita. She put her ear next to her mouth. She puts her fingers on her wrist. She shakes her head.

3 December, 1943 — "Why did Mama die, and we haven't?" Rivka asks.

"I wish I knew."

"I don't get it! We were also diagnosed with Typhus," Ira says.

"We'll see… Some people die, some people don't," I say.

"What did Mama do to deserve this?" Rivka asks.

"Come here, Rivka, Ira. Hug me. I love you both more than anything."

"I love you, too, papa." Rivka says.

"I love you," Ira says.

"Your mama didn't do anything to deserve this. She was a kind, loving woman. What happened, happened.

There is nothing we can do. We must go on living our lives without her."

Rivka finds a job in a flower store during the day. In the evening, she sells roasted sunflower seeds near a movie theater.

The next nine months are a blur of sorrow and depression. I work my shifts as a security guard with a heavy heart, missing my beloved Ita.

Droves of lonely women in Kattakurgan seek to comfort me and to find comfort in me. I'm not interested.

Rivka becomes adept at arranging flowers while working at the flower shop. She makes a few rubles selling sunflower seeds in the evenings.

Boys show interest in her, but they are younger— mere children—and don't do anything for her. The boys her age or older are all soldiers fighting the Germans, far from Kattakurgan.

Ira hangs out with a group of boys his age, and they play soccer and cards. In the summer they swim and fish in the Zeravshan River.

Fourth Movement
CHAPTER 53

24 August, 1944 — "Kishinev has been liberated from the Germans! You may now go home."

We hear this announcement on the radio, and while the war is not over completely, for people like us—from Moldova—there is much rejoicing in Kattakurgan.

The factories begin a slow re-tooling back to civilian use while people from places that have been liberated are encouraged to return to their hometowns and help with the effort to rebuild.

Hershel, Sarah, Rivka, Ira, and I pack up our possessions—including our tents—and put our affairs in order in preparation to return home. I go to the closet in my bedroom, remove the wall panel, extract my savings, and carefully stow it in my travel bag.

1 September, 1944 - The day before the train is scheduled to depart, Rivka, Ira and I go to the Jewish Cemetery to visit Ita's grave as we have many times since she died.

We each place a small stone on the simple marker that says, "Ita Kaplan Gershovich. 9 March 1903 – 2 December 1943."

"I don't want to leave mama here," Rivka says.

"I know baby. It's terrible," I say.

"I miss her so much," Ira says.

"We all do, but we have to keep living," I say.

"But she's buried here," Rivka says. "I'll never get to visit her grave again."

"She'll always live on in our hearts. She would want us to see our dreams come true."

CHAPTER 54

14 September, 1944 - The family and I board a northbound train out of Kattakurgan with all our worldly goods stuffed in the overhead rack and in bags at our feet. We are among thousands of refugees—more than two-thirds of the wartime population of Kattakurgan—who are leaving the city.

Rivka hands me a dry bread roll from among the food that includes dried fruit and nuts that she and Sarah have been hoarding—go figure—since we received news of our impending departure. Here we go again.

As the train heads north, Rivka swallows a mouthful of fruit and says, "I can't believe it was four years ago that we reached Uzbekistan by crossing the Caspian Sea from Baku. That was so awful!"

"The whole nightmare has been one long blur. Ugh!" Ira says.

"The Russians built this direct line, straight north from Kattakurgan and then west to Mother Russia to expedite transport of tank parts and munitions," I say.

"This should get us home much faster," Rivka says.

"Faster is a relative term," I say.

Rivka makes a sad face and puts away the food to make sure it lasts beyond the first leg of our trip. It takes us thirty-six hours to get to Guryev, Kazakhstan, which is on the mouth of the Ural River, at the north shore of the Caspian Sea.

All the way, the temperature hovers around 37 degrees Centigrade, and we have many moments when we aren't sure if we can endure the heat, the endless vibrations, or the swaying, not to mention the din and stench of our fellow passengers.

All we know is that this is only the beginning of the trip. I monitor everyone, making sure they at least have enough water; Sarah rations our meager food supplies, and, thank God, nobody has lice. Rivka and Ira amuse each other when they aren't annoying each other, playing games and planning what they will do when they get home, wherever that might be.

This we endure for *six excruciating days.*

CHAPTER 55

20 September, 1944 - When we arrive at the Kishinev Central Train Station, I fantasize that cousin Leo and Aunt Rosa will be there to meet us. Instead, the station is a ragged, scorched shell of its former self, just like most of Kishinev. Some masonry walls still stand, but there are almost no roofs, windows, or doors.

The sky is gray. Birds are flying south, and the leaves that remain on the linden, oak and walnut trees are mostly brown. Once we are out of the train car, I look at the people in the streets and in a refugee camp that is growing in the park across the street.

After all the horror and the stops along the way to Kattakurgan, this almost feels inviting, like home.

Dark clouds in the sky bode the possibility of afternoon thundershowers, but not being a newcomer to such a situation, I assess our options and take inventory of our possessions. With everyone's help, Herschel, Ira and I doing the heavy tasks. We hurriedly claim a rectangle of dirt near the corner of the park and pitch our tents under a tree.

Rivka and Ira collapse onto their backs on a patch of grass.

From this campsite, I watch the stew of humanity, which prominently includes the Soviet Auxiliary Police in black uniforms who patrol the city.

Later, two officers wearing brown uniforms with green epaulets march by in knee-high leather boots, and Herschel whispers, "From what I gather, they're NKVD—the interior ministry of the Soviet Union that acts as police."

"What's the difference between the officers in black uniforms and the ones in brown?" I ask.

"I don't know," Herschel says, "but they're making one thing abundantly clear: the Soviet Union is in control."

After the officers are out of earshot and the kids return from an exploratory stroll, Hershel says, "Look at us. Before the war, we owned a thriving business, a nice home, income property, and a good life. Now we have nothing."

"We have each other. You have Sarah and I have Rivka and Ira," I say.

"I know the war isn't over, but God I hope Shimon and Yakov are still alive," Herschel says.

"Don't forget Grandpa and Grandma Gershovich," Rivka says. "And Grandma Kaplan."

"Dvora," Ira says.

"Leo, Anna, Aunt Rosa, everyone we knew… Please, God," I say.

There is a long silence as we watch other refugees light kerosene stoves, adjust their tents, and scrape together food.

Herschel rubs his eyes and says, "Being here in Kishinev, everywhere I look—despite all the carnages committed by the Nazis, the Romanians and God knows who else—I still get transported back to the Passover weekend of 1903. This place still gives me the creeps, because I can't get out of my head the unspeakable atrocities that were perpetrated during the pogrom."

I HATE CHRISTIANS. I HATE GERMANS. WHY DOES EVERYONE HATE JEWS? WHY IS THERE SO MUCH HATE IN THE WORLD? HATE. HATE. HATE.

After dark, lots of people talk. Children cry, and there's a general clamor of people camping in the park; our latest vestige of home.

In the distance, we hear a lone violin, which stirs within me the yearning for music. As a result, the will to live—maybe even love—regenerates in my soul.

In the darkness, Rivka asks, "What's the name of this place again?"

"Kishinev. Kee-shi-NEV," Ira says. "The capital of Moldova."

"Ugh."

CHAPTER 56

21 September, 1944 - The next morning, after delicious, dried bread and dried fruit for breakfast, Herschel and I exchange looks and I ask, "What do you suppose became of our old home and store?"

"I was wondering the same thing," Herschel says.

"Are you ready? Can you handle it?" I ask.

"No. But let's do it anyway."

"I've never seen it, or I was three and don't remember. I'm game," I say.

I make sure nobody is watching me, discretely pull some cash out of my bag, and stuff it in my pocket. I glance at Rivka, and she non-verbally acknowledges that she will guard it.

Herschel and I set out into the wreckage of Kishinev. No trolley busses are running yet, so we walk north along Albisoara Street, following the path of the railroad tracks and the Bic River.

Twenty minutes later, we come to the intersection of Ismail Street, where we turn right. Herschel stops in his tracks, overcome with emotion. Kitty-corner across the street is the former site of *Gershovich's Hardware and Tack*, on which neither of us have laid eyes in forty-one years. I was three, and Herschel was five.

"Here we are," I say.

Herschel nods. "I swore I would never return."

We enter the front gate in silence. The trees are charred skeletons, while here and there are small piles of bricks and cobblestones. Mostly, the place had been picked clean, but the two-story living quarters still stand—minus a wall here or part of the roof there—and are in nearly livable condition.

We enter, pass through the empty living room, and walk down the hall to the largest bedroom. I can see that Herschel is very uncomfortable.

"This is where it all happened?" I ask.

"To Dvora, Aron and me." Herschel points up the stairs.

"How did they kill Dvora and Aron?" I ask.

"I don't know. If I did… I can't get that memory to surface… and that's probably a good thing. I'm sure it was gruesome," Herschel says.

"It must have been right here where that… awful man snapped your leg?" I ask.

"Yes… *That*, unfortunately, I can't forget," he says.

"And up there," I point upstairs, "is where… they threw me off the roof?"

Herschel nods, suppressing tears.

"And Mama?" I ask. "Something horrific happened to mama, didn't it?"

Hershel closes his eyes. "They…"

"What?" I ask. "I don't want to know, but… I need to."

"I was barely old enough to understand what happened… but, unfortunately, I do… and until now, I have blocked it from my memory and have never spoken of it to anybody," Herschel says.

"What happened? Please, tell me," I say.

"They… gang-raped her," Herschel says.

My jaw drops in disbelief.

Herschel continues, "I don't know how many of them, but they tied papa to a chair and made him watch… and… she got pregnant… and terminated it…"

I'm engulfed by a wave of emotions. Finally, I say, "That explains…"

"What?" Herschel asks.

"Why mama and papa didn't have sex," I say.

"No way. What?" Herschel asks.

"That's what papa told me on our trip to Bolgrad," I say.

"Get out of here."

"He said that once women have kids, they don't want sex. I didn't want to believe him. This provides a bit more explanation as to her… brokenness."

I hug my brother and we sob together, but at the same time feel a sense of catharsis. "Mama survived… at least to raise us as children," I say. "And we survived. Here we are. We have to go on living."

After a long silence, Herschel says, "I'm glad we came. I needed to see it." He begins to tap a rhythm on his chest, then looks up and asks, "Do you want to go to the Jewish cemetery and find Dvora and Aron's graves?"

"I couldn't handle it right now," I say. "Perhaps another time. We have the rest of our lives to come to terms with this."

"I agree," Herschel says.

"Now, I want to find out what's left in Kalarash," I say. "Maybe we can move back there and not stay in this awful place."

"Ugh," Herschel says.

Herschel and I walk back toward the camp. When we are across the street from the train station, I say, "Go on ahead. I'll be back at the campsite in a few minutes. I want to check something out."

Herschel nods his head and disappears into the tent city.

I cross the street, go up to a ticket window where there is an attendant, and say, "Excuse me, is it possible to take a train to Kalarash?"

The attendant gives me a grim look. "No. The tracks on that route are mangled. It could be months."

"Thanks for the information," I say.

Turning around, I walk to the street. I look right, then left at the tent city across the street, take a deep breath and head southeast toward the Botanica District of Kishinev.

At Decebal Boulevard, I'm not sure where I am going, but I instinctively veer right and continue another half a kilometer through a residential area until, on the right, I come to a huge park with lots of mature oak and linden trees surrounding a lake. Geese land in a lake as I continue south, and I squint at what looks like stairs and maybe some kind of ancient ruins on the shore of the lake. Before long, I come upon several horses grazing in a corral surrounding a white house and a barn.

I walk up to a brown horse standing near a wooden fence. As I pat a white patch on its nose, a bow-legged man in black overalls hobbles out of the barn. I smile and wave.

The man takes off his hat and scratches his gray hair. "Is there something I can do for you?"

"Actually, there is. I'm looking to hire a horse and carriage."

"You've come to the right place."

"And I need a shovel."

Half an hour later, I return to the refugee camp driving a horse and buggy. Rivka spots me when I am half a block away and runs up to greet me.

As I park the carriage, Rivka pets the horse's neck. "Beautiful horse."

"Isn't he?" I jump off the buggy and hug her.

"Makes me miss Ruth," Rivka says. "I wonder what happened to her."

"Something good, I hope," I say.

"Wow!" Herschel says as he and Sarah come out of their tent and see my ride. "Where'd you get that?"

"Down here in Rose Park. I found a stable and managed to hire this horse and carriage for a few days," I say.

"Why?" Sarah asks.

"I want to go to Kalarash. I can't go by train."

"There probably is no Kalarash," she says.

"Then again, maybe there is. I'm going to see for myself," I say.

"Suit yourself," Hershel says.

"You're wasting your energy," Sarah says.

"We're going to end up here," Hershel says.

"I would rather keep the image of the Kalarash of old in my memory," Sarah says.

"Fine, I'll go by myself," I say.

"I want to come," Rivka says.

"Okay. We'll be gone for five or six days," I say.

"I'm good with that," Rivka says.

"Get packed," I say, then I go inside the tent to do the same.

As Rivka's about to follow me into the tent, she looks at Ira, who resembles a rag doll lying on the grass.

"See you when you get back," Ira says.

CHAPTER 57

23 September, 1944 – Rivka and I clip-clop into Kalarash, up Strada Alexandru cel Bun, and past the heavily damaged Kalarash Train Station. The shtetl is deserted.

Our hearts sink. Neither of us says it, but we're both thinking the same thing. Any shreds of hope that mama and papa might have survived are diminished.

Whole blocks are burned to the ground. A few chimneys stand, and blackened trees cast spooky silhouettes against the sky.

A kilometer later, we reach the remains of our former home and *Gershovich's Hardware and Tack*, which has not been spared from fire. A few walls still stand, though, along with the chimney.

Rivka tiptoes through the ashes to where the kitchen was. "This is where mama and I made so many meals."

I feel forlorn as I pace about, awash in memories.

Rivka saunters to the corner of the kitchen that she and Ita used as a studio, picks up part of a picture frame and the charred remains of a painting, and says, "This was an Austrian landscape." She runs her fingers over the oil brushwork and tears up.

Looking to the sky, I fall to my knees and begin to cry. "Oh, Ita, I miss you so much."

Rivka kneels next to me, we embrace, convulse in grief, and tears flow.

"And what happened to grandpa and grandma? And Grandma Charna?" Rivka cries.

"Maybe they escaped somewhere and will eventually turn up… We may never know," I say.

"Aunt Riva, Uncle Rachman, Cousin Bene, Fania, Tanya and Alya? My God, is most of our family… gone forever?"

I shrug and shake my head. We both cry and hold each other for a very long time, until, at last, I stand up and help Rivka to her feet.

Rivka blows her nose on a handkerchief and says, "Okay, Aunt Sarah was right. There's nothing here, so let's go back to Kishinev."

"Not so fast," I say, and I go to the buggy, fetch the shovel, and make my way to the backyard.

"What are you doing?" Rivka asks as she follows me.

I don't answer, but instead, take two paces from the corner of the house and began to dig.

After about five minutes, I start to feel concerned.

"What are you looking for?" Rivka asks.

"I'll tell you when I find it. Hmm. It's deeper than I remember." I keep digging. The pile of dirt next to the hole grows, sweat drips down my brow until at last, the shovel hits something metal.

"Ah-ha!" I look around to make sure nobody but Rivka is watching. I keep digging, and soon unearth a green metal box.

I use my thumbnail to unclasp a hook, open the lid, and bare my teeth.

Rivka gasps as I reach into the box and pull out a bottle of vodka. "We came all this way for vodka?"

I snicker, I reach in again, and slowly pull out a big, fat wad of cash and after that, other treasures.

Rivka squeals and jumps up and down. "Now I see why we had to come back."

I give her a big hug. "This will go a long way toward getting our lives going again."

"Yes! I dare say. Good job, papa. You're amazing. I love you so much." She hugs me again.

"I love you, too, Rivkale." I touch the tip of her nose.

Spontaneously, I start singing a song that has been brewing in my head, "In one small town they named Kalarash, a blessing called Rivkale, beautiful maidele, laughed and cried and made sweet hamentashen. Sings like in fairy tales, spins like a *dreidele*.

"Nice lyrics! We'll have to work on that song," Rivka says.

"We will," I say, and I keep humming it as we walk around the property and check our *podval*, which, by no surprise, has been raided and is completely empty.

Disappointed, I'm about to suggest we go back to Kishinev, but something behooves me to take one more walk through the remains of the house.

As if by an unseen force, I'm drawn to the steps to our basement. Rivka, clinging to my shirt tails, follows me down the charred steps. My mind's eye goes back to the days leading up to the German invasion, and in the dim light, I walk across the basement to a closet in the far corner. I open the door and I can't believe my eyes when, there before me, is my violin.

I pick it up and embrace it... almost as if Ita has returned from the dead.

After securing the cash box, vodka, shovel, and my violin on the buggy, Rivka and I climb on. I lift the buggy whip, make a "sK-sK" noise, and as if the whip were a conductor's baton, I tap the horse on the rump and urge it into a gentle rhythm.

South of town we come upon a farm I had noticed on the way in. We hop off the buggy and look around. "God, they burned everything."

I roll my eyes and shake my head as we walk around to the back of the house, where we see two wooden doors leaning against a mound of dirt.

"No. The Germans couldn't have missed this," I say.

I grab a handle on one of the doors and pull. It won't budge.

"Hang on," Rivka says, running back to the buggy and fetching the shovel. Upon her return, she says, "This might help."

I take the shovel and push the head under the bottom of the door, using the shovel for leverage. After pushing and pushing, finally we hear a CRACK!

Cool, musty air wafts out as we swing open the door and climb down into a dark hole in the ground. As our eyes adjust, we see that the walls are lined with shelves stocked with jars of beets, peaches, apples, and all sorts of other preserves.

"Awesome!" Rivka says.

We empty the *podval* and load its contents onto our cart.

26 September, 1944 – It's late afternoon when Rivka and I roll into Kishinev, practically un-noticed. We look like just another Jewish guy and his daughter driving down Lenin Prospect with a load of refuse, but in our heads, there is music—new hope for the future.

On our left, we pass the Nativity Cathedral, which is eerily empty and horribly bombed. No bells toll from the belfry. On our right is Stalin Square, a public garden where the monument to Alexander Pushkin stands un-toppled, but most of the trees are burned and bomb craters pock the unkempt grass that is overrun with weeds.

The tent city has grown considerably in just the five days we've been gone.

As we approach our campsite, Ira runs out and greets us. "You're back!"

Sarah and Herschel poke their heads out of their tent.

"Thank God," Sarah says.

I motion with my finger for Herschel to come to the buggy, and as he approaches, Rivka and I dismount. "Don't make a big fuss but look at this," I say. I discretely lift the burlap bag concealing the contents of the buggy, and Herschel's eyes almost bug out of his head.

"And what's more," I say as I dramatically lift a tarp and reveal my violin, "we're back in the music business."

"Yes!" Herschel says. "I found two sticks and a couple of buckets—drums. We've got a band!"

Rivka and Sarah quietly fix dinner for the family, and we all eat better than we have in years.

Over dinner, I tell them the visual details of our trip to Kalarash—the bombing, the devastation and what remains—but I omit what we found and what we unearthed. I pour Herschel, Sarah, and I a spot of vodka.

"So, nothing is left for us there?" Herschel asks as he takes a sip of vodka.

"Not nothing," I say and go silent. I make sure nobody is watching or listening, then quietly reach into the bag I am clutching at my side.

"Look what else I dug up in Kalarash," I say, and reveal the thick wad of money. "Before we left, I buried this under the store."

"I guess it's time for us to make something happen," Herschel says.

"And wait, there's more," I say.

I pull out my violin, which I had cleaned and tuned as best I could on the journey from Kalarash, considering the age of the strings. I clutch it under my chin, lift my bow, and launch into a rendition of Hava Nagila. Everyone sings and dances along, including many camps next to us.

With music back in my life, I willingly—even eagerly—resume my role as the family's conductor, leading us from our sad song back to a new, happier normal.

Change is slow but steady throughout Kishinev. The red Soviet flag flies over city hall. A crew cleans the statue of Lenin. More streets are renamed. But food, housing and other necessities remain scarce.

Over me—and all of Kishinev—hangs a sadness for the past, a mourning for the people, especially for Ita and my parents, plus the buildings and everything destroyed during the war.

Rivka and Ira enroll in high school, resuming their educations taught exclusively in Russian, which isn't a problem, since that's mostly all they spoke in Kattakurgan.

Herschel and I put our names on a list to get an apartment.

I land a job managing a shoe factory.

Herschel finds employment as a security guard.

Sarah, as always, is there as our stage manager, and continues to hope her boys will return.

Night after night we sleep in our miserable tents in the park.

Each night, it gets colder.

When I'm not working, I wander the residential areas of Kishinev, looking for a way to finagle a place to live.

"We'll freeze if we wait for the government to issue us an apartment," I say.

Construction is going on all over Kishinev. Many former single-family houses are being divided into smaller units, and I have my eye on one in a formerly Jewish neighborhood.

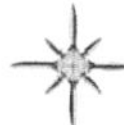

CHAPTER 58

3 November, 1944 - I walk past the house I have been eyeing as painters work on the interior trim.

I approach one of the painters who has a long beard. "Excuse me. Are you in charge of this building's renovation?"

"Yes," says the man, who has string hanging from his undershirt. "This used to be my house. The government is going to let my family live here. Isn't that kind of them? But I have to divide it into three units."

"When will they be finished?" I ask.

"Could be a couple of weeks. Probably more like a couple of months," he says.

"Are all of the units spoken for?" I ask.

"Two are, but I'm not sure about the middle one," he says,

"I want it," I say.

"Yeah, uh, so do a lot of people," he says.

"Maybe so, but… I've got some money," I say.

"How much?"

"How much will it take?"

11 November - Three weeks later, Ira and I and tear down our tent in the park across from the train station.

Along with Rivka, Herschel, and Sarah, we carry our belongings to our new apartment.

CHAPTER 59

1945 – Winter ticks by long and painfully slow in Kishinev.

I always show up on time at the shoe factory.

Rivka and Ira attend school and study hard.

Herschel guards a factory.

Sarah, shops, cleans the apartment, and cooks meals. And prays for Shimon and Yakov.

8 May, 1945 – Almost eight months after our return to Kishinev, People all over the Soviet Union hear on the radio, *"Vinemanye, vinemanye, gahvoreet Moskva."*

"Attention, attention, Moscow is speaking!

The instrument of unconditional military surrender has been signed by the German armed forces.

The war is over.

There is much rejoicing.

27 May, 1945 - A group of soldiers pass in their green fatigues. Herschel stands and waves at them. "Excuse me! Do any of you guys know Shimon or Yakov Gershovich? Have you seen them?"

The soldiers shake their heads.

CHAPTER 60

16 February, 1946 - On a snowy Saturday I walk up Armenian Street to the market to hopefully buy something decent to eat for dinner. The birch trees are barren, the ice and slush on the path are dingy, and two measly vendors shiver outside the market, with one selling potatoes that look rotten, and some marginally better heads of cabbage. The other sells eggs, and watches over five cages clucking with live chickens next to a bloody chopping block.

Chicken and cabbage. Again. Rivka and Ira will be delighted. Maybe I can get some sausage inside. I take a deep breath and try to cheer myself up. It beats subsiding on raw corn and apples and sleeping on the sidewalk someplace unpronounceable enroute to Uzbekistan.

Oy.

I select the best-looking head of cabbage and say to a craggy woman who sits on a chair, bundled in a heavy coat and a black headscarf, "I'll take this."

As I pull part of my dwindling reserve of cash from my pocket, suddenly, I make eye contact with… a woman. A curvy, attractive woman, who is about my age wearing black pants, a gray head scarf, and a black-wool overcoat. Somehow, I detect a familiarity with this woman with wavy brown hair and brown eyes… my repeatedly broken heart refuses to risk excitement.

We make eye contact. One, two, three… We smile. One, two, three… My heart and mind cling to their broken state.

The queue advances, and she disappears into the store.

"Five kopeks," the vendor says.

I pay the vegetable vendor then turn my attention to the weathered man who attends the chickens, who I've known since early on when I returned from Uzbekistan. No one else is waiting. "Please butcher one chicken," I say, as I point into one of the cages, "that one looks pretty healthy, and I'll take ten eggs. I'll pick them up when I come out of the store."

"Okay, no problem."

I cinch up my bag of potatoes and cabbage and, luckily, the end of the queue no longer spills into the chilly outdoors. I enter, and perhaps by divine intervention, I position myself right behind – dare I say it? – the vision of loveliness I beheld earlier, third in line, who radiates the essence of femininity.

As I study the menu scribbled on a chalkboard behind the counter and make a mental list of what I will buy, the woman glances back at me and grins girlishly. She looks vaguely familiar.

I push my glasses up on my nose and take in her cushiony vision. She loosens her headscarf—it's a bit stuffy in the store—and while I can't say my heart has healed from the loss of Ita, I feel hints of my desire for female companionship.

"And so, it is in this post-war Soviet republic, it's like torture to stand in line for sausage," I say as if I'm reciting Pushkin. "What are you hoping for today?"

She stiffens in surprise at the sound of my voice, which I find odd. Then I hear her voice.

"Milk, feta and hopefully some sausage."

She removes her head scarf, turns and at last I get a full look at her face.

"What are you hoping for?" she says.

My heart almost leaps out of my chest. "You!"

"Elazar?" she says.

My jaw drops, my mind swirls. "It cannot be!"

She starts crying.

"Mariam?" I say as tears begin running from my eyes.

She nods, and we fall into each other's arms.

At this point, everyone in the store is looking at us, though these kinds of reunions are what everyone is wishing and praying for. On occasion, they do happen. Like right now. To me.

"No way. I can't believe it!" I say.

"Neither can I. How is it possible that you're alive?" she asks.

"Flat feet and near-sightedness, just for starters. And… I don't know where to begin. A lot of luck."

The line advances.

"How about you? I haven't seen you since… that night. I'm so sorry about what I did to you," I say.

"It wasn't your fault," she says.

We stare into each other's eyes, holding hands. The line advancers again.

"How'd you end up here?" I ask.

"Oh, God. That's a long story," she says.

"You don't have to tell me. I'm sorry, I don't mean to pry," I say.

"Let's just say this is where I ended up after the war," she says.

"Me, too. We, uh, spent most of the war in Uzbekistan," I say.

"Ugh," she says.

"Yeah. Not exactly the garden spot of Eastern Europe. Or is it Asia?"

A wave of grief from the loss of Ita swells through my being.

"I can only imagine the horrors you faced," she says.

"Yeah."

The woman in front of us points at what she wants but keeps changing her mind.

"Where did you spend the war?" I ask.

"I ended up in Astana, Kazakhstan," Mariam says.

"You singular? What happened? You were married. Your parents disappeared," I say.

She tells me how her husband and son were both drafted into the Russian military, and how she hasn't seen either one of them since. In Kazakhstan, she met up with a Russian officer… then he got killed.

"How about you?" she asks.

"Ita, my wife, passed away… of typhus in Kattakurgan," I say.

"Oh, God. I'm so sorry," she says.

"It was really awful. But I have a daughter who is nineteen, and a son who is sixteen," I say.

"You're lucky to have them," she says.

We make eye contact, and I feel a tingling sensation in my loins as I inhale the smell of her perfume. I clear my throat and she gives me a warm smile. Chemistry radiates in our eyes and in our touch, as if not one second had passed since that night in the wine cellar.

"Where are you living?" she asks.

"Right down the street on the corner of Armenian and Bucharest. And you?" I ask.

A troubled look comes over her as searches for the answer to this question. She opens her mouth to speak when the attendant behind the counter says, ""Next!" The woman in front of Mariam leaves the store, and she steps up to the counter.

I go home and fix a batch of chicken and cabbage soup. I set the table with a new spring in my step.

I feel like a teenager, trying to find the right moment to tell my kids what happened to me today.

"What? You've been acting funny all evening," Rivka says.

"I met someone," I say.

"That's great!" Rivka says.

"What's her name?" Ira says.

"What's she like?" Rivka says.

"Her name is Mariam. Gabashvili," I say.

"As in the vintners from Kalarash?" Rivka asks.

"Yes. We knew each other many years ago."

Neither bats an eye. What happed between us was before they were born.

"Her husband died during the war. We have a lot in common. I think we like each other," I say.

"I'm very happy for you," Rivka says, but a very sad look on her face betrays her happiness. I know what she's thinking.

"This has to be a tough time to be a young woman," I say.

"I wish I could meet somebody," Rivka says.

"I have Golda the yenta working on it for you. It's tough," I say.

"Talk about bad timing. I get to spend my high-school years in fabulous Kattakurgan. Now I come to marrying age right after the war, and almost all the guys my age are dead," Rivka says.

"Rivka, listen to me, you will find someone. And Ira, when you are old enough, you will too. But you need to know something, and you need to hear it from me. I met Mariam many years ago and fell in love with her, and I wanted to marry her."

"Why didn't you?" Rivka asks.

"Papa forbade me to marry her because she wasn't Jewish. I'm not kidding. He said if I married her, he would disown me."

"Why?" Ira asks.

"In one word? Hate. Christians hate Jews, Jews hate Christians. Hitler, Germans, Romanians, Italians hate Jews. Kill them all! It's a big part of what this war was about. But now I have a choice to make. Papa isn't around to stop me, so despite all the horrors we've been through, I will not let them defeat me, and I will not let hate overcome beauty in this world."

THE END